BLOOD TIES

A JOHN JORDAN MYSTERY BOOK 16

MICHAEL LISTER

PULPWOOD PRESS

Print ISBNs:

ISBN-10:1-947606-02-6

ISBN-13:978-1-947606-02-9

Join Michael's Readers' Group and receive 4 FREE Books!

Books by Michael Lister

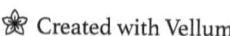

HOW TO READ THE JOHN JORDAN BLOOD SERIES

The Blood Series

This *New York Times* bestselling and award-winning series features a conflicted detective—a cop with ties to Atlanta who also works as a prison chaplain in Florida. He's a man of mercy and justice, compassion, open-mindedness. He's also a smart, relentless detective.

The John Jordan mystery series is character-driven and realistic—thoughtful mystery thrillers involving the hero's journey of a good man trying to be even better, as he helps others along the way.

Like John Jordan, the author, Michael Lister, was a prison chaplain with the state of Florida before leaving to write full-time.

If you're new to the John Jordan series, you can begin with any book, but we recommend one of these 3: *Power in the Blood, Innocent Blood,* or *Blood Oath.*

Power in the Blood, the first fiction the author ever wrote, was published over 20 years ago, and though it's recommended, the books in the John Jordan series don't have to be read in order.

All the books in the series are novels—mystery, thrillers,

whodunits—except for the 3rd book in the series, *Flesh and Blood*, which is a collection of short stories featuring temporal and metaphysical mysteries. If you don't care for short stories, feel free to skip *Flesh and Blood* and continue with the fourth novel *The Body and the Blood*.

If you decided to skip the short stories and continue on with the novels, we recommend that you read the short story "A Taint in the Blood" in the book *Flesh and Blood* to find out what happened to Laura Matthers from *Power in the Blood*.

The 7th book in the series, *Innocent Blood*, is a prequel going back to John's very first investigation. Though the 7th in the series, it can be read 1st or 7th since it's a prequel.

The 10th book in the series, *Blood Cries*, is the second in the "Atlanta Years" series within a series following the 7th book *Innocent Blood*. It can be read 2nd or 10th.

The 17th book in the seres, *Blood Stone*, is the 3rd book in the "Atlanta Years" series within the series following the 10th book *Blood Cries*. It can be read 3rd or 17th.

John Jordan is an ex-cop in books 1-10, but once again carries a gun and a badge beginning with book 11, *Blood Oath*.

All of the John Jordan novels are available in high quality hardback, paperback, ebook, and audio editions.

Interspersed throughout the "Blood" books there are other related books that are part of the John Jordan universe. These books are extremely important to the series and provide essential backstory for characters, connections, and locations of series regulars. Most of all they answer the questions most readers want to know. They include *Double Exposure, Burnt Offerings, Separation Anxiety, Thunder Beach,* and *A Certain Retribution*. These are "Blood Series" books without being John Jordan Mysteries.

We hope you will enjoy all the books in the John Jordan series and eagerly await each new entry.

Be sure to join Michael Lister's Readers' Group for news, updates, and special deals on the John Jordan series.

I n the early morning hours of July 4th 2017, an unimaginable murder took place in a rented Gulf-front mansion in a gated subdivision of Cape San Blas in Gulf County, Florida.

There were no signs of forced entry and only six people were known to be in the house at the time—nine-year-old Mariah Evers, Mariah's dad, the Atlanta rapper Trace "Evidence" Evers, his girlfriend, Ashley Howard, Ashley's ten-year-old son, Brett, their nanny, Nadine Wade, and Trace's best friend, manager, and Mariah's godfather, Irvin Hunter.

While this unsettling and disturbing deed was taking place, being discovered, and being investigated, I was away for my wedding, as happy as I've ever been.

And I wasn't the only member of the Gulf County Sheriff's Department away at the time.

Sheriff Reggie Summers was out on medical leave.

From the initial 911 call, our depleted department mishandled the critical early hours of what would become one of the most shocking and perplexing cases in our county's history.

Every step and misstep was seen and shared, seen and shared, by the world's interconnected web of audio, video, and pictures, as the media, both reputable and not, descended onto our unprepared and ill-equipped little area like a swarm of black flies, exploiting both Trace's newfound fame and the shock and sensationalism of the murder for something as hollow and transitory as ratings.

Trace wasn't yet a household name like certain rappers who had been gunned down or featured in films or married musical royalty, but he had a couple of solid hits and had appeared on the first season of Donald Glover's popular and critically-acclaimed FX TV series *Atlanta* in a not insignificant four-episode arc that had elevated the once-regional rapper into a promising and possibly bankable entertainer.

In what seemed like hours, local, regional, national, and even a few international news outlets were reporting, often inaccurately, about the most bizarre and salacious elements of the surreal and unsettling case as clips of Trace's concerts, TV appearances, and a music video featuring Mariah ran in loops beneath them.

Mariah had been featured in his latest music video for a song he had written for her—and the footage from the shoot turned out to be the final ever filmed of the nine-year-old who was murdered in a locked house in a gated community while on vacation with her family in Florida.

The talented and happy Mariah Elizabeth Evers, who seemed to have her entire life ahead of her, wouldn't even get to see her tenth birthday.

For these and other reasons, including some remarkable similarities, the murder of Mariah Evers became almost immediately and indelibly linked to the disquieting death of another young girl whose disturbing and haunting unsolved case had earlier this year reached the heartbreaking milestone of its twentieth anniversary.

2
___

I find Reggie alone on this dark, rainy night in her living room, recuperating on the couch. And I'm grateful I didn't have to see her mom when I arrived.

Since moving back to Wewa with her son, Rain, Reggie has lived with her mom in a mobile home on the Apalachicola River —a mobile home modified because of where it sits so the entire back wall of the living room is nothing but windows that look out onto the wide river.

I know I will eventually encounter Sylvia Summers, but I am not looking forward to what I know will be an awkward and intense interaction.

"I can't believe this happened when we were both out," she says.

"How are you feeling?"

"Better before this happened," she says. "I'm actually meant to be returning to work in another day or two."

Reggie and I were both shot during the same river swamp shootout a while back, but she was shot far more and far worse than I was and then had to deal with a wicked infection as the result of her wounds.

She adds, "That means we get to clean up this mess together."

"Look forward to it," I say. "What do you want me to do between now and when you return?"

"I want you to go home and get a good night's sleep. Then in the morning I want you to review the entire case, everything that has been done so far, all the evidence, look at it with a fresh set of eyes."

"Arnie won't like that."

Arnie Ward is the investigator who caught the case.

"I don't care what Arnie Ward likes," she says. "No way I'm not gonna have my best investigator working a case like this. Besides . . . he shouldn't have bungled the case."

Arnie was called in by the on-call deputy who was first dispatched to the scene. And though he immediately phoned Reggie and began to get her input on what to do and how to proceed, he made a few costly investigative mistakes during the first crucial moments.

"Would we say *bungled*?" I ask.

"Don't know about *we*, but *I* might," she says. "What were you thinking?"

"*Mismanaged* maybe?"

"Don't know yet, do we? We'll have to see what we see, but from where I'm laying, I think *mismanaged* might be just a bit too generous."

I shrug and glance down the dark hallway leading to the bedrooms at the other end of the trailer.

"She's asleep," Reggie says.

"Who?"

"Mom."

I nod.

"You dreading seeing her?" she asks. "Regretting your decision?"

Though the answer to both questions is *yes*, I shake my head. "Just too tired for it tonight."

She nods her understanding. "She won't get up."

I had recently agreed to keep a secret for Reggie and her mom that now I wasn't sure I could.

"We haven't really talked about it," she says, "about your decision and —"

"We will," I say. "Just not tonight."

Through Reggie's back windows lightning flashes, illuminating the rain falling on the river, and the river in the rain, backlit by the lightning, appearing even more mysterious than it normally does at night.

"Still can't believe what was done to that beautiful little girl," I say, shaking my head, continuing to look out into the rainy night.

"It's the most disturbing and shocking murder I've ever been this close to, and I don't want you to think I'm losing sight of that —I mean by talking about the case itself. I don't want you to think that that's all I'm thinking about."

"I don't. Never would. Know you too well."

"Thing is," she says, "it's because of what happened to her and my desire to get the sick fuck who did it that I'm so bothered by how badly the case has been handled."

"I know."

"My biggest concern is that it has been fucked up beyond repair. I'm wondering if we'll be able to salvage the case and get a conviction at this point. The thought of the guy getting away with it because of what we did or did not do is just too . . ."

"We'll get it sorted out. Won't stop until we do."

"I'm not just talking about figuring out with a reasonable certainty who did this to her, I mean being able to make a case and punish the prick."

"I know. We'll get there."

Neither of us says anything and the rain on the roof seems to grow louder.

"How are Daniel and Sam?" she asks.

"Going home to find out now. Merrill and Za stayed with

them while we were away. I dropped Anna off at my Dad's place in Pottersville to get the kids and her car and came straight here."

"Oh shit. Forgot to ask. How was your wedding? Sorry I wasn't able to be there."

"It was . . . everything we wanted it to be. It was . . . It's hard to imagine it being any better."

"I knew it would be. Just like the marriage. I'm so happy for you, John."

"Thank you. When are you going to make an honest man out of Merrick? Where is he, by the way?"

"Where do you think? Workin' on a podcast about Mariah. Pretty sure he wants Daniel to help with it soon as he's able. They'll be part of the media feeding frenzy we're having to deal with on this one. Means I'll be sleeping with the enemy."

I smile.

Before Daniel Davis went missing, he and Merrick, Reggie's significant other, hosted a true crime podcast together called In Search of. They were working on In Search of Randa Raffield when Daniel vanished. During Daniel's absence, Merrick has continued the podcast, which has grown even more popular—though some of the podcast's most vicious trolls have accused Daniel's disappearance of being something the two men staged as a ratings stunt.

"You think he will be?" she asks.

"The enemy or sleeping with you?"

"Meant Daniel. Think he'll be up for that kind of thing again?"

"I'm about to go find out."

3

As I had hoped, I get home in time to help Anna put the girls to bed—something we linger in doing because we've missed them so much during our short time away.

In an ironic role reversal, it is us trying to get them to stay up a little longer and them wanting to be left alone to drift off into peaceful sleep.

When we finally relent and retreat to our own bedroom, we ignore the bags waiting to be unpacked and collapse into our bed.

"You know the only thing better than being away on honeymoon with you?" I say.

"What's that?"

"Being in our home with our girls with you."

She smiles. "I'm so happy to be home."

We had spent the past few nights on some pretty plush hotel beds, but none could compare to our bed in our room in our home.

I slide over toward her and we meet in the middle of our firm kingsize. She lays her head on my chest as I put my arm around her, caressing every part of her I can reach.

Outside the rain tings on the metal of the window unit and

thumps the soggy soil of our backyard. Inside, we both nearly simultaneously release a contended sigh.

"Did you talk to Sam or Daniel?" I ask.

Sam Michaels, an FDLE agent I had worked with and Daniel's wife, had been staying with us while he was away. She had suffered a gunshot wound to the head on a case we had worked together, and though her prognosis had not been good, she's surprising everyone but those of us who know her best with her miraculous recovery.

Since Daniel's return, and because of his own need for healing and care, they have both been staying with us, though they are scheduled to move out this week.

"He was doing PT with Sam when I got home," Anna says. "I just waved and said *hey* but didn't really get to talk to them."

"What'd Dad have to say?" I ask. "Everything go well with them?"

Dad and his new wife Verna had kept Johanna and Taylor for us while we were away. Having surprised us with the announcement that they had eloped shortly before our wedding, they have been married only marginally longer than we have.

"Everything went extremely well. Normal stuff. Taylor ran a little bit of a fever—probably getting another tooth—and Johanna has a bit of a cough. But the far more interesting thing is where I found them."

"Oh yeah?" I ask. "Where's that?"

"Well it wasn't at their house."

"Really?"

"They were here. Jack and Verna came here to help Daniel with Sam."

"What happened to Merrill and Za?"

"That's the even more interesting part," she says.

"We inspired them to run off and get married?" I ask.

"Negatory. How'd your talk with Reggie go?"

"Fine. She's better. Just worried about how the case has been handled and if we can salvage it."

"That poor, poor child," she says. "There's some unimaginable evil in this world, but there's nothing more evil than . . ."

I nod and pull her even closer to me, feeling certain that she's doing what I'm doing—thinking about our own girls being brought up in such a world.

"Who does Arnie think did it?" she says.

"The dad. Trace."

"That's what I figured," she says. "This should be interesting for you."

"Whatta you mean?"

"That's where Merrill went," she says. "Trace's defense team hired him to investigate and provide protection."

After leaving corrections and doing some community organizing work and mentoring, Merrill had started his own security and investigations agency, and though he had provided security for a few celebrities on Panama City Beach and Black's Island before, this would be by far his most high profile case to date.

"Really?" I say. "Trace already has an entire defense team? And Merrill is on it?"

"You and Merrill ever been on the opposite sides of an investigation before?"

4

I find Daniel at the kitchen table.

He's eating a bowl of cereal.

Sam is asleep in her hospital bed in the corner of the living room. Anna is asleep in our bed. The girls are asleep in their room. We alone are awake.

The house is quiet and dim, the only illumination coming from the small light above the kitchen sink.

I sit down across from Daniel and glance over his shoulder through the picture window to the wet front yard beyond.

"Want some?" he asks, nodding toward the open box of cereal in front of him.

His voice is soft, night-quiet.

I shake my head. "Thanks. I'm sure there's some real food around here somewhere if you'd rather have—"

"This is fine," he says. "Just wanted a little something before bed."

Bed for Daniel these days is our living room couch, which he has pulled next to Sam's hospital bed.

"How're you feeling?" I ask, my voice low and a little dry.

Anna and I had dozed off and I'm still a little groggy.

He shrugs. "Not sure. Still sort of out of it."

He slides the cereal box over so it's no longer directly between us.

"Kinda numb," he adds. "It's still like I'm like way down inside my body, looking up, looking out from a distance. Disconnected. Kinda cut off."

I nod.

Since returning to us, Daniel has been quiet, withdrawn, disoriented, lost.

"Please don't feel in a rush to leave," I say. "Y'all are more than welcome here for as long as you need to be. Make sure you're ready before you—"

"Look at your living room," he says. "It's a disaster."

I turn and follow his gaze, looking over my shoulder at the rectangular room that resembles an open bay sick ward more than a residential living room.

"Looks fine to me," I say, turning back to toward him. "We love having y'all here and want y'all fully recovered before you . . ."

"Thanks, John," he says. "I can't tell you how . . . I'll never be able to thank you and Anna enough for all y'all've done for us."

"Just don't rush."

"I really don't know what's wrong with me," he says. "Why do I still feel so . . . off? Why can't I remember more of what happened?"

Since being back, Daniel has had very little memory of his time away, recalling only vague images and impressions.

I'm sure drugs were used on him, but none were found in his system when he was tested while in the hospital for dehydration and observation when he first returned.

"Anything else come to you while we were gone?" I ask.

He shrugs. "Few things, but . . . I can't know if they're memories or dreams or . . . hallucinations. Like the others . . . they're unlike any memories I've ever had before."

I wait.

Though there is still milk and cereal in it, he slides the bowl and carton of milk to the side next to the cereal box.

"This time . . . I didn't just remember Randa being there. There was a man too. But . . . I don't know. I think I'm . . . I think it was a hallucination—then or now or both. He doesn't seem real."

If Randa had help it would explain how she had been able to do all she has—including taking and controlling Daniel.

"Did he seem threatening? Dangerous?"

He shakes his head.

"Do you have a sense of his relationship with Randa?"

He shakes his head again. "He's all distorted in my foggy, addled images of him. They both are. It's like one of those old B films, the low budget black and white pictures that had the scenes that depicted a guy on a bad drug trip—everything doubled and floating, voice distorted, images demented. It's like that. Feels like it can't be real."

I nod.

It has stopped raining now, but raindrops continue to fall from the trees, catching the light of streetlamps and glistening as they do.

"Tell you what is real," he says.

"What's that?"

"The guilt I feel," he says, glancing over at Sam.

A gust of wind ripples through the huge oak limbs and the shaking leaves release a torrent of rainfall beneath the branches.

"Why guilt, do you think?" I ask.

Given the manner in which Daniel disappeared, we had wondered if he had perhaps gone willingly. Had he found himself attracted to Randa and wanting to escape a life of caring for his invalid wife for what seemed at the time the rest of their lives?

He shrugs and frowns and looks down as his eyes begin to glisten. "Not sure exactly. Just . . . leaving Sam when she's . . . or was the way she was."

"Did you leave her?" I ask.

It's the most pointed question I had asked him since his return.

He looks up at me, his eyes narrowing into a question.

"Of course I—what do you mean?"

"Did you leave her or were you taken?"

"You askin' if I went willingly?" he says.

"Did you?"

"You know I didn't know it was Randa at the time," he says.

I nod.

"We connected, really hit it off. I was lonely and she was so . . . smart and energetic and so . . . alive. And my wife was . . . mostly dead."

I nod again. "I know."

"I was attracted to her, pulled to her in a way I hadn't been to anyone other than Sam," he says.

"I don't know anyone who wouldn't understand the temptation," I say.

"But I never, not for one moment, ever considered doing anything that would betray my vows to my Sam or dishonor her in anyway. And it certainly never crossed my mind to leave her. Not even for a nanosecond during one of those random crazy thoughts that come out of nowhere and mean nothing."

I nod and smile, and before I know what I'm doing I'm standing up and moving to his side of the table and wrapping him up in a hug.

As I do, he breaks down and begins to sob.

Unable to be quiet any longer, he sobs so loudly it wakes Sam up, and I release him and he rushes over to her, leaning down on her bed so she can hold him as he cries.

As I ease out of the room to give them the privacy this

moment demands, I can see that she's sobbing too—probably the most therapeutic experience either of them have had since their long nightmare began on a dirt road down near Crystal River a little over two years ago.

5

I crawl into bed next to Anna physically exhausted and emotionally drained.

She rolls on her side and backs up toward me and I fall asleep in my favorite position—spooning the woman I love.

Dreams come immediately.

Vivid, lifelike, disturbing dreams of JonBenét Ramsey dance across the stage of my subconscious in colorful, feathery, sequined pageant dresses.

Other girls and mothers waiting in the wings.

As a hooded-eyed child molester in the audience licks his lips, the tip of his too-small tongue dryly darting out of his misshapen mouth.

Jump cut to December 25, 1996 in a rambling remodeled sprawling house on 15th Street in Boulder, Colorado. A lit Christmas tree in every room. The remnants of Santa's visit still strewn about the house. Quiet. Peaceful.

Silent Night. Holy Night. Moments before a vicious assault, a violent brutalization, sexual savagery, the death of beauty and innocence. And there's nothing I can do about it.

I can feel myself trying to wake up, but I'm unable to escape the noxious nightmare.

Scream of a child.

Helpless.

She is helpless.

I am helpless to help her.

I wake in a cold sweat, racing pulse in my throat, feeling frustrated and embarrassingly powerless.

Sliding my arm out from beneath Anna, I slowly and quietly roll out of the bed, slip on my shorts and t-shirt on the floor and steal out of the room.

The first thing I do is look in on the girls, lingering a few moments to listen to the sweet sound of their breathing.

Then, padding down the dark hallway, I ease into the kitchen, glancing over to see Daniel and Sam sleeping in the living room.

Slipping over to the cabinet and removing a glass, I fill it with water from the tap and stand at the sink sipping it while attempting to slow my breathing and heart rate.

Through the wide window I can see the wet world, puddles on the driveway, standing pools in the front yard, oak leaves glistening, the window itself dotted with raindrops.

Up beyond the old Wewa Hardware building, across Highway 22, the lights of the laundromat shine extremely bright in the dark night.

The building was once and for many, many years a convenience store. Now it holds a fishing tackle and bait store called The Fishing Shack on one side and a no name 24 hour laundromat on the other.

When the owner remodeled the building into two store fronts and rented them out to the two new businesses, he had installed the brightest lights in town beneath the cement covering of the small front porch—lights that actually partially illuminate our front yard nearly a block away.

As I'm wondering what the electric bill must run, I see him.

Sitting there inside the building, a scope in his hand, is Anna's ex-husband Chris Taunton.

I take a step back from the window, duck down and attempt to watch him without him seeing me.

Holding a magazine as if he's just waiting for his clothes to finish drying, he occasionally lowers it and brings up a rifle scope out of his jacket pocket and glasses our home with it.

Stepping into the mud room and slipping my shoes on, I walk out through the garage and run across my neighbors' backyard.

The grass of my neighbor's mostly neglected yard is high and wet. I run along the still and dark Lake Julia, random raindrops fall from limbs and leaves.

In a few moments, I reach Highway 22 down near the Dixie Dandy—the small grocery store, gas station, and deli in the old, converted, dilapidated patchwork building on the same lake as our home.

I'm far enough down so he can't see me.

I cross the empty highway. American flags adorning the light poles lining both sides of the street hang damp and motionless above me.

The small, sodden town appears abandoned, stores closed, streets empty. The July night is hot and humid. There is no wind, no movement. Only the red and yellow flash of the traffic signal at the intersection of 22 and Main.

Running along the small unpaved alleyway, I come up on the side of the building, around the ice machines humming in the quiet night, and along the front porch.

Standing behind a Coke machine situated between the two storefronts, I am able to observe Chris without him seeing me.

He's the only person in the laundromat. For all I can tell from here, he could be the only person on the planet.

He's seated on a black plastic chair in front of a bank of dryers. Beneath him the flecked and speckled tile floor is the same one the convenience store had forty years ago.

I step over and snatch open the door, the fresh, clean smell of detergent and fabric softener wafting over me.

He jumps up.

"Sit down," I say.

He holds his hands out in a placating gesture. "Okay, okay," he says. "Don't shoot."

He's always making statements like that. It's just more ironic tonight since I'm in shorts and a t-shirt without a weapon of any kind—or even a cellphone.

Overhead white ceiling fans turn slowly, out of sync with the spinning dryers behind him.

"I can't even do my laundry anymore without being harassed?" he says.

"This isn't harassment and you know it. Hand me the scope."

His eyes flash wide for a split second, but then he recovers and shrugs and shakes his head. "I use Tide to wash my clothes. If you need mouthwash to hide the liquor on your breath before you go home to my wife and child, 'fraid I can't help you."

"You know I wasn't talkin' about mouthwash," I say.

I extend my hand toward him.

"Give me the rifle scope you've been using to watch our home with now," I say.

He shakes his head. "I don't have a—"

"Why're you wearing a jacket in July?" I ask. "It's hard to imagine a more hot or humid night."

He shrugs again. "I'm cold natured. That a crime now too?"

"Do you have a weapon to go along with that scope or just the scope?" I ask.

"I'm unarmed," he says. "You think I'd be stupid enough to walk around your town with a gun? Not that it matters much. Y'all can just plant one on me after you shoot me, can't you?"

"Tell you what," I say. "All I want to do is sit down beside you and have a little talk. That's it. But before I do, you're going to take off your jacket and hang it on that rack over there. Okay? That's not too much to ask. Besides, think about how much more comfortable you'll be."

He studies me.

I hold out my hands and turn around. "Look," I say. "I'm unarmed. Don't even have my phone on me. I just want to talk."

He frowns and nods, then stands, shrugs out of his coat, and hangs it on the galvanized rack a few feet away.

When he sits down again, I sit beside him.

"I've worked with a lot of criminals over the years," I say. "A lot. Both inside and out of prison."

"That's nothing to brag about."

"The ones who never learn, never change, are the ones who justify and rationalize everything they do and truly believe themselves to be victims while they are victimizing others."

"You should write a book," he says. "A murdering drunk home wrecker gives advice to criminals."

"Thing is," I say, "you got away with murder."

"I've never gotten away with anything in my entire goddamn life," he says. "And now I've lost everything. Check that. I had everything taken from me—most of it by you, the motherfucker dispensing advice in the laundromat in the middle of the night."

"You could turn your life around," I say. "It's not too late. You could take the opportunities you've been given and make a new start."

"*Opportunities*?" he says, his voice rising. "I never realized just how fuckin' funny you are, John. When you lose your current job, you should consider standup."

"Everything you're doing is self-destructive," I say. "I know you wish me ill. And I'm sure there are others you're hoping to harm, but the end of the road is your own destruction—no matter who else you injure or kill along the way."

"Please look at me with a straight face and tell me you care about me," he says.

"I care about my wife—the woman you tried to kill," I say.

"I never tried to—"

"I care about her."

"She was my wife at the time," he says.

"I care about your child—evidently more than you do."

"Why do you think I'm here?" he says, his voice rising again. "It's because I love them both that I'm sitting here watching your stupid house. That's my family over there in that house. Mine. Not yours."

"I was trying to appeal to your own sense of self-preservation," I say. "Trying to get you to see that no matter who else you harm, you're going to inflict the most pain upon yourself. Call it care—for you or for those in your wake."

"My family. Mine. I sit here all alone in the middle of the night in this piece of shit Podunk town and spy on my fuckin' family because you stole them away from me."

"Okay," I say. "But ask yourself this. When I got shot a little while back . . . if that had been fatal . . . if I had died and was out of the way . . . you and Anna would be back together, you, her, and Taylor would be one big happy family?"

6

"I know everyone blames me, "Andy is saying, "but I don't know what else I could've done."

Andy Finch is a large, soft man with thinning blondish hair and flat blue eyes. He was the on-call deputy on Cape San Blas when the call came in and was the first to respond to the scene.

Because Cape San Blas is relatively small, only one deputy is assigned there during the season. During the offseason, Cape San Blas shares a deputy assigned to other parts of the area.

"I did everything by the book for what it looked like it was," he says, "and every one of these damn Monday morning quarterbacks blaming me for what happened would've done the same things. No, that's not true. Most of 'em wouldn't've done half of what I did."

I nod. "I'm not here to blame you. I know how fluid and difficult these situations can be. I had something similar happen when I was a patrol officer in Stone Mountain."

Wanting Andy as relaxed and unguarded as possible, I'm meeting with him on his day off away from the department. We're standing beneath an enormous oak tree in the front yard of the Methodist church on Main Street where Andy has been mowing the grass. In fact, he's still sitting on the large yellow zero turn mower at the moment, the motor ticking and clicking as it cools.

"You did?" he says.

I nod. "So I understand, but it's not my job to evaluate what you did or why. I'm not here to second guess or criticize you. And nothing you say will jam you up."

Beneath his large frame, the mower looks smaller than it actually is, and when he shifts his weight the seat groans and the metal structure below it moans.

"The sheriff has asked me to look at everything we have so far," I say. "Run a fresh pair of eyes over every aspect and element. That's all I'm after."

He nods and seems to relax a little more.

The morning traffic on Main is slow and intermittent—and about the only thing stirring any of the thick, humid air around.

We're in the midst of the wettest North Florida summer I can ever remember, and though it's not raining at the moment, the sky is giving every indication that it will be again soon.

"Will you take me through everything step by step?" I ask.

He nods. "If that's what the sheriff wants."

"Thank you."

Even beneath the shade of the giant oak limbs on an overcast morning the heat is stifling, and I can feel the sweat trickling down my brow and back.

"The call came in," he says. "Dispatch said some parents vacationing at Stars Haven woke up to find their daughter missing and a note that said she had run away. So I was responding to a runaway situation. And I did it by the book. Took me a few minutes to get in. I called up from the gate but no one answered for several minutes. At the time I didn't see that as suspicious. Just figured they were looking for her or upset, out of sorts, or something."

Stars Haven is a small Gulf-front gated community with the largest and most luxurious mansions on the Cape.

"We're talking about people with a lot of money," he says. "Staying in probably the safest place there is. I had no reason to suspect that this was anything other than what I was told it was. And it wasn't just that I was told what it was. Everything I saw confirmed what I had been told."

From the black shingled roof of the tall redbrick church building, chimes began to play—the first chimes of the day, announcing it was ten in the morning. We waited for a moment for the loud gongs to finish so we could hear each other again.

I glance around at the tall grass and feel bad for keeping Andy from his second job. With as much rain as we've been getting there's no way he's been able to keep up with his regular accounts.

"I'll be honest," Andy says, "I was surprised by how young the couple was and how they looked."

"Whatta you mean?"

"They looked too young and too . . . I don't know exactly . . . to have enough money to stay in a mansion like the one they were in."

"Tell me more about how they looked."

"He's black. She's white. I learned later he's some sort of rapper. And that's what he looks like. Also didn't know at the time that he's an ex-con, but I could tell. He has the eyes. And the woman . . . well . . . between you and me . . . she looks sort of low rent. I don't know. I'm just telling you my honest observations."

"That's all I want. Don't edit or clean it up. Just give me your unvarnished impressions and observations and tell me exactly what happened. I'm not recording this or even taking notes. This is just between us."

He nods. "The dad and the . . . woman. They're not married and she's not the girl's mother. Not sure what to call her. Anyway, they meet me at the door. The woman, Ashley something, is holding the note. Soon as she sees me she hands it to me."

I had read the note this morning. A copy of it is in the murder book. It is written in a child's hand that was matched to Mariah's writing and reads: *Dear Daddy, Ashley and Brett or to mean to me. I love them but cannot stay. I sorry for leaving you like this. Yall all will be happy with out me. Please do not look for me. I will be fine. I will miss. Love you, Mariah.*

"Told me they found it in her bedroom when they went in to wake her up," he says. "Said she had put pillows under her covers the way kids do to make it look like they're still in bed. I ask them to show me where they found it and told them I needed to do a full search of the house. They said they had already done that, but I told them I had to do it. I'm sure you know the statistics. Something like half of all kids who run away do so because of conflict with their parents, because the parents encouraged them to, or some sort of abuse—sexual, physical, verbal. I didn't take their word for anything and I maintained a healthy suspicion about everything throughout. They asked me to hurry, said every moment counted and we had to get out there and find her. I told them I understood, but there was a certain way these things had to be done, a way they work best, that we did them for a reason, and I was going to do everything just by the book. So they took me to the girl's bedroom—which took a while. I've never been in a house that big before. It was huge. I then searched it, which took a long time, room by room—every closet, every bathroom, every nook and cranny. They were impatient and rushing me the whole time, telling me I needed to call for more help and get officers on the streets searching for her. I followed procedure. I searched the entire house. You tell me, given what I knew at the time, did I do anything wrong?"

I shake my head—something I would've done even if I thought he had done something wrong.

"They kept saying, 'we're just here for the holiday. We're renting this place. Mariah doesn't know anyone. Doesn't know her way around. We've got to get out there and find her.' I then asked them for a picture. Have you seen her?"

I nod.

"She's a very, very pretty little girl. Or was. 'Course mixed girls are always some of the most beautiful."

Many of the people around here—and I guess other places too—used the term *mixed* for biracial children, and though it's extremely common and I truly believe most of them don't mean it as a pejorative, I've never liked it. It's probably just me, but the term seems to carry a negative connotation—almost like half-breed—and I just don't like it.

But Andy's right. Mariah Evers was a truly beautiful little girl. Flawless features. Mocha skin. Mesmerizing green eyes. Long, dark, thick wavy hair.

"Now that I've finished a search of the house and have a picture of her, I go outside and began to look around the exterior of the house, through the neighborhood, and along the beach," Andy says. "Since it's a gated community, I figure she could easily still be inside it. Either way, I don't think she could've gotten very far. 'Course I don't know how long ago she left. Was it the night before or that morning? So . . . here's what I was thinking. You tell me if I'm wrong. I do a search of the area—with the parents, the nanny, and the manager, who were also there. Maybe we find her and that's the end of it. If we don't, I have to figure out if we think she's still in the area. If she is, I'll get the K-9 unit out here and search for her, as well as get robocalls going in the neighborhood and surrounding area. If none of that works, then we escalate it and activate an Amber alert."

I nod. "Sounds solid to me," I say, though I question how much time he's taking with each step.

"As we're searching around, I see this kid watching us from the next mansion over. I mean . . . he's not just watching, he's . . . he's not taking his eyes off us. And the way he's looking . . . I know something's up. I ask Miss Nadine, the nanny, who he is. She says his name is Caden Stevens that his family is vacationing here from Montgomery and that he and Mariah and Brett have played together some. He's maybe eleven. Brett is ten, and Mariah is nine —but hell, from what I gather she's more mature than both of them. Was, I mean. So . . . here again this is a judgement call, but I take the time to go over and talk to Caden. *Have you seen Mariah this morning? Do you know where she is? Did you know what she was planning?* And I can tell he's lying to me. He knows something. So what do I do? Do I interview him, press him on what he knows? Do I call for the dogs? I did both."

"Hard for anyone to argue with that," I say.

"Oh, you'd be surprised. But anyway, I figured, hey, it's gonna take a while to get the dogs out here—I mean out to the Cape. They're coming all the way from Gulf CI, so I make the call and while I'm waiting for them, I interview little Caden."

7

L arge raindrops begin to fall and we dash over and take shelter on the front porch of the church. The porch, like the steps leading up to it, is smooth, bare concrete and holds up the tall white columns that hold up the high overhang.

"Lived here all my life," he says. "Never seen so much rain in one summer."

I nod and look out at the huge old bell mounted on the sign in the front with the Methodist cross and flame on it, the fat raindrops splatting hard on the black metal surface.

"Caden's a good kid," he says. "You can tell. "Respectful. Good manners. Sort of quiet and shy. Has a gentleness about him. Wasn't a formal interview or anything, so I just spoke to him outside of the house, kind of informal like. Didn't ask the parents' permission and they weren't present at first. He told me he liked Mariah a lot. Enjoyed hanging with her a lot more than Brett. Swore he had no idea where she might be. I had a hard time telling, but I felt like he was telling the truth and keeping things from me. Figured if we didn't find her soon, he'd warrant a second, more formal interview."

I thought the same thing while reading his report and noted that Caden hadn't been interviewed again and had returned home with his family to Montgomery, Alabama.

"I wasn't even really finished talkin' to him when I see Ashley and Trace over in their rental talking very animatedly into their phones. I tell Caden I'd like to talk to him again in a few minutes and walk over to see what's going on with Trace and Ashley. When I ask what's happening, Trace gives me nothing but attitude. Says I'm moving too slow, not taking it seriously. Said if he was white or Mariah wasn't mixed I'd have my fat ass in gear. He was off the phone by now, but Ashley was still on. Told me she Googled what to do when a child goes missing and it said after reporting it to local law enforcement, call NCMEC and report it to them and that's what she was doing."

NCMEC is the National Center for Missing and Exploited Children.

"Said while she was doing that, he called his lawyer and publicist and had them contact the FBI and the media," Andy says. "I felt like I had just stepped on a landmine and it was just a matter of time before it blew me to bits. I ask them to come back inside with me. I wanted to call Reggie and let her know what was going on before she saw it on her damn TV set. If I made a mistake it was here. After my little chat with Caden, he and his parents sort of followed me over to Trace's and then a few other people gathered and when we went inside, they came in too. 'Course I didn't know it was a crime scene. Didn't know anything but that there was a little girl who left a note and ran away."

"There was no way for you to know it was a crime scene," I say.

He frowns, shrugs, and nods. "Since we had an hour until the dogs would arrive and all these people wanting to help, I told them to divide up in teams of two or three and start searching the area, beginning at Stars Haven and moving outward. While they did that, I called Reggie and told her what was going on. Even though she was on medical leave I knew she would want to know —given everything, including the money and fame of the dad involved—which is why I was gonna do it anyway, but with them calling the damn FBI and the media, I knew she had to know and the sooner the better."

I nod. "You were right to call her."

"She said I should've done it sooner."

I smile. "She'd have to be completely incapacitated not to want you to call as early as possible with something like that."

He shrugs. "Yeah, well . . . I called very early in the process."

I nod.

"Anyway, so everybody's searching as we wait for the dogs and more people arrive—some of Ashley's family I think."

According to the murder book, Ashley Howard grew up very poor in Wewa—where most of her family still lives. At seventeen she got pregnant by Justin Harris, a young man from a wealthy family in Port St. Joe. The two had a short, tumultuous marriage, but had figured out a way to coparent pretty well over the years. In fact, Justin, who's a real estate agent on the Cape, is who Trace and Ashley used to book their rental in Stars Haven.

"Trace and his manager—an ex-con named Irvin Hunter who was staying in the house with him—kept berating me for not doing more, said they were gonna have my badge, questioned why I didn't care more and concluded it was racial. Most of that came from the manager. Self-important prick. Trace . . . seemed, at least at times, genuinely upset and sort of lost, and others . . . like he was acting—saying and doing what he thought he should. I don't know . . . take it for what it's worth. That's just my observation and we both know how often those can be wrong."

"Did the additional people—Ashley's family and others—join in the search or . . ."

"Ashley and Trace stayed at the house while the others

searched. So did the manager and the nanny—and of course Brett was somewhere around. So when the family got there—and it was just the mother, a brother, and a sister—they stayed at the house with Ashley, didn't join the search. 'Course they were all over the house. I just didn't know enough at the time to keep them from . . . I wish I had treated it like a crime scene. I should have. I'm not sayin' I shouldn't, but . . . given what I knew, what I had been told and presented with . . . I made the best decisions I could."

"I know you did. So what happened next?"

"Since we were just waiting I decided to make the most of the time and get as much information out of everyone as I could. Told them they could really help me by answering honestly and telling me anything they could think of. I asked about any conflict or problems between Mariah and anyone in the family. They said there was none. I reminded them of what her note said, and they said there had been an adjustment period since Ashley and Brett had been around more. Mariah got less of her daddy's attention and Ashley took on a more parental role. But nothing major. Nothing to warrant any of this. What about Mariah's mom, I asked. They said she has absolutely nothing to do with her, that she's an addict and toxic person and lost custody back when Mariah was very small. Any other friends or family in the area she might go to? They said no. All her friends and family were in Atlanta. Everybody was on edge—even Ashley's family that had just gotten there. Lot of nervous energy in the room. Tension. Lot of the interaction was intense—and not just with me, but with each other. I got the sense that Ashley's family embarrassed her and she wished they weren't there. Don't think Trace wanted them there either. But Irvin, the manager, ran interference for him, and Trace kept leaving the living room where we were, disappearing for a while. Guess he was walking off his nervous energy or something. Anyway, wasn't much interaction between him and Ashley's family."

"How long was Trace gone at a time?" I ask.

He shrugs. "Not too long. Longest time was probably ten minutes. Most of the time it was a lot shorter—like five or three. He wasn't in there when the other note was found."

The *other note* is the ransom note that changed everything.

"Ashley's mom, Arlene," he says. "Arlene Lafontaine was telling a story about the time Ashley ran away as a child when Nadine the nanny came running in the room screaming. She was holding a piece of paper in her hand, sort of flapping it around. As she's bringing it over to me, Trace rushes into the room and snatches it out of her hand. 'What is it?' I asked. She said it was a ransom note she found in Mariah's room. Trace, who was reading the note, lost it. Threw a glass ashtray through the glass top coffee table. Everyone else started panicking. The whole scene was pandemonium."

According to her statement, Nadine went into search Mariah's room again and decided to make up the bed while she was there. As she did, a ransom note fell out of a fold in the bedspread.

It read: I'll make this simple so even an ignorant thug like you can understand. I have your daughter. If you want her back it will cost you $250,000.00. That's a very small amount because I want to do this fast and easy. I know you have a lot more, but that's all I want. I'm not greedy, have no desire to be nigger rich like you. I don't want no gold teeth or spinning rims or any shit like that. Your song says you will never leave her again. Well, maybe not, but she's left you. You say you will never hurt her again, never let her down. We will see if you really mean that. I don't want to hurt your little girl. Don't make me. Just gather the money and I'll call you with where we'll meet to make the trade. Don't test me boy. Don't call the police. Don't tell anyone. You do and it's lights out for the little mixed girl. Just get the little chump change together and wait for my call. Be smarter than you seem and don't fuck this up. Your little girl's life depends on it.

"What'd you do then?" I ask.

"Cleared the house," he says. "Got everyone out, which wasn't easy. Put the note in a plastic evidence bag—even though three or four of us had already touched it. And called the detective on duty, Arnie Ward. From that point forward, all I did was secure the scene and wait for the cavalry."

8

Our home is visible from the Methodist church on Main Street.

So the entire time I had been talking to Andy, I had not only been keeping an eye on our house, but missing Anna and the girls and wanting to be with them.

After concluding my conversation with Andy, I swing by the Dixie Dandy and grab Anna's favorite breakfast food from the deli and surprise her with it.

While Daniel does physical therapy with Sam and the girls play in their room, Anna and I have a picnic on the floor of my library.

My library is unlike any room I've ever had in any previous house. It's in the converted formal living room in the front corner of the house. Floor-to-ceiling bookshelves line three of the four walls. The fourth has glass enclosed shelves of the barrister variety with my signed first editions in them. They are shorter shelves and stop about three feet from the ceiling. Their tops are filled with art objects and family pictures, behind them framed photographs hang on the wall.

"This is *so* good," she says, crunching on a piece of crispy bacon. "So sweet of you. Don't you want some?"

I shake my head. "Just want to watch you enjoy it."

Though there are a couple of chairs, we are as usual sitting on one of the two large rugs on the center of the hardwood floor.

"How'd it go with Andy?" she asks.

I smile and shake my head again. "No shoptalk," I say. "Not now. Let's just enjoy each other and the food. I do want to talk about the case with you—especially once I know more. Maybe tonight. I was thinking . . . I'd really like to get Sam and Daniel involved somehow."

She nods vigorously, finishes chewing and swallowing and says, "I *love* that idea. And I love no shoptalk right now too. But let's extend that to no household or kid talk too."

"How'd you sleep?" I ask. "How do you feel?"

"Slept great. Feel good. Even better now that my honey paid me a surprise visit with bacon."

"I told you when you married me there would be bacon."

"I guess I just took that to be sexual like most everything else you say to me."

"Sometimes bacon is just bacon."

"You sayin' if I lock the library door and we manage to get a few more uninterrupted minutes, I won't get lucky?"

"I am not now, nor I have I ever been, saying anything of the dang kind."

"We are still on our honeymoon, aren't we?"

I nod emphatically. "Least for another fifty years or so."

"So we're sort of duty bound, wouldn't you say? Sneak in and check on the kiddos without them seeing you while I savor these last bites and when you come back, lock the door."

Johanna and Taylor are playing happily and intensely, and when I return to the library and lock the door, Anna and I do the same.

When we are finished, I say, "Why thank you, Mrs. Jordan."

"My pleasure, Mr. Jordan. You know how much I love to score on the library floor."

Once Mariah's body had been discovered, Arnie Ward, the investigator who caught the case, had been partnered with an African-American FDLE agent named Lakeisha Colvin, but when Andy Finch first called in the cavalry, Arnie alone rode in.

Arnie is in court today, so we meet during his lunch break.

Arnie Ward is a decent man and a solid detective. Conscientious and hardworking, he plods along checking the boxes, filing the reports, crossing the t's and dotting the i's of each case. He has a small, limited tool box—one without creativity or intuition—but the tools he has he uses often and efficiently.

There are people in this world who do not look like what they really are. Arnie isn't one of them. His average build, clean shave, clear eyes, barbershop haircut, drugstore aftershave, sensible shoes, and utilitarian clothes offer no conflict or contradiction to the soul or mind of the man beneath them.

"Sure wouldn't've hurt my feelings any if you'd've caught this one instead of me," he says.

We're sitting on the tailgate of his white F-150 on the side of the courthouse beneath the only shade we can find, taking advantage of a few moments without rain.

"To be honest," he says, "I'm glad you're lookin' into it now."

Unlike many of the men I meet in law enforcement and virtually every other field, Arnie isn't egotistical or interested in recognition, and I know he won't be defensive as we discuss the case.

"Case like this . . ." he says, "is too important, too complicated to be left to just one detective. I'm glad we have agent Colvin and I'm glad we have you."

"Thank you," I say. "I appreciate that. And I'm not here to second guess or be critical of anything that's been done. Just trying to gather and evaluate the information, not the investigation."

He nods.

Between us, a series of plastic Tupperware type containers hold a wide variety of homemade dishes that appear far too fresh and sophisticated to be simple leftovers.

Arnie is also the kind of man who brings his lunch every day.

Each morning, his wife prepares a full, large meal for him and places it in a complex array of plastic containers, and each day at lunch, Arnie sits at his desk and eats every bite.

"Sure you don't want some?" he asks.

The container he's holding and eating from now appears to have some sort of Salisbury steak with a thick brown gravy and mashed potatoes. A smaller container with the lid off balances precariously on his lap and has steamed vegetables that he stabs and eats in between bites of the meat and potatoes.

I nod. "Thank you."

"Okay, so . . . I'll make this quick 'cause I don't have much time. Judge wants to finish the case today, which is all right by me. I drove out there, wondering what was really going on and if I should call in the FBI or FDLE or what. No reason to if she was still in the area, but if she had been taken out of the state and this thing was going to involve several agencies and jurisdictions, we'd need them. The call I made was to wait until I got out there to see what we had. I should have called Reggie at that point, but I thought Andy Finch had, so I didn't. But I should have anyway. She's right to be mad at me about that. Hell, I shoulda called Langston at least and he would've called her, but . . . I was so focused on what I had to do, on what I was going to be dealing with."

Langston Costin is the Chief Deputy, who has been in charge since Reggie has been out on medical leave.

"Turns out . . . I didn't make the wrong call exactly," he says. "We didn't need the FBI because we really didn't have a kidnaping, but . . . if I had called Reggie sooner—or Langston—they would've probably called in FDLE crime scene lab from the beginning. Would've been helpful to have them there sooner."

I nod.

Before us, the courthouse is busy—citizens coming and going, conducting their business with the court, the clerk, the property appraiser. Out on 71, as vehicles pour into town, most of them with Georgia and Alabama tags on them, they slow as the road widens and the two lane highway becomes the four lane parkway. They slow, but not nearly enough.

"By the time I got out to the scene, Andy had it taped off and everybody out," he continues. "The parents and their staff and family and friends were at a neighbor's house next door. It's funny to think of them as neighbors—they're all just renting these places for the holiday, but . . . you know what I mean. It was the house of Mariah and Brett's little friend, Caden. Andy hands me both notes—the runaway and the ransom. I read them both. And I was just . . . overwhelmed. Honestly, I was like . . . this is beyond me. Thankfully, the K-9 unit got there just before me and were already at work. I knew I needed to get with the dad, Trace . . . and make sure he had his phone, get the recording device attached to it, see who his wireless provider was so I could contact them about a trace on the call when it came. As I walked over to the house next door to talk to him and do that, I started to call Reggie, but I got a call and then I was there and talking to the dad and . . . it was a while before I called her."

"Was Trace cooperative?" I ask.

"Extremely," he says. "Respectful. Helpful. Anxious to do anything he could to get his daughter back."

"That's interesting," I say. "Think Andy had a very different experience with him."

"He was upset and intense, but . . . just what you'd expect."

"So you get the recording device hooked up and contact the cell provider," I say.

He nods. "And there was no call," he says. "For a ransom, I mean. He got other calls, of course. Some of them . . . You should listen to them. Some sounded pretty suspicious to me, but . . . no ransom call."

He pauses a moment to eat the final bite of the container he's working on, close the lids, and open the final one—some type of cobbler with a crunchy top layer on it.

Dark storm clouds gather out over the Gulf to our west reminding us that this briefest of respites from the rain can't last much longer.

"I wait with the family for a while," he says after a few bites of the dessert, "but there's no timeframe on the note, so we have no idea how long before the call will come, so I go back outside to check on Andy and the K-9 unit and to call Reggie. But once again . . . things happen fast and I don't call Reggie right away, so even more time passes. Nearly the moment I walked out, the correctional officer in charge of the dogs—I forget his name—"

"Ronnie Wyrick?" I say.

"Yeah, that's it. Ronnie. He comes over to me and says there's no scent outside. He doesn't think the little girl ever left the house."

"What was he using for scent?" I ask.

"Pair of shorts and a t-shirt she had worn just the day before," he says. "The stepmom—Ashley, I mean, picked it right up off the floor of Mariah's bedroom. It was fresh. Ronnie said the dogs . . . I don't know . . . he could tell by the way they reacted that there was plenty of her scent on it."

I nod and think about it.

"He said his dog keeps going to the back door—the one on the first floor that leads out to the pool deck and he wanted to know was it okay for him to let the dog go inside. On the lead, of course, he'd be right there with him. I said sure. And he said he wanted me to go with him . . . in case . . . he found something. I said sure, okay. And instead of calling Reggie, I went back in the damn house with Ronnie and the dog. But letting the dog go in the house and not calling Reggie were the least of my mistakes at this point. See, with Andy over at the entrance guarding the perimeter and me going with Ronnie . . . there was no one with the family over at the neighbors'. And evidently Trace was watching us from a window 'cause . . . I didn't know it at the time, but . . . he must've seen us around the back door and then go in. Like I say, I didn't know it at the time. So we go in and . . . and remember we're talking a big ass house. It's built up on stilts with parking underneath like most houses that close to the water and then there are three levels above that. Hell, the pool isn't in the ground. It's on a platform so that it's level with the first story deck. Anyway . . . huge house, but the dog doesn't spend much time in the living room or kitchen—a little, but then he's off, climbing the stairs, Ronnie on the lead behind him and me behind him. There's a guest bedroom on the first floor with the living room and kitchen and game room and all. The manager was staying in it. The second floor held the master suite. Trace and Ashley were staying in it. The third floor had three rooms—a kids room and two guest rooms. Mariah was in the kids room, Brett was in one of the guest rooms and Nadine the nanny was in the other. You could tell the dog was alerting on her scent sort of all over the house, but it went straight up to her room. Which, I mean, that's what you'd expect, right? So I didn't think much of it. I . . . I searched the house personally. Every room. I knew the . . . I knew she wasn't in the house. I just figured her scent was the strongest in her room so that's why he was going there. But when he got in there . . . he alerted on her bed. The bed she slept on. There was her bed—just sort of a regular bed with a big pink comforter on it with pillows beneath it and a set of bunk beds on the other wall. The bunk beds were made up, looked like no one had been on them at all, but her bed was unmade, the comforter hanging half off down to the floor. This is the bed where both notes were found—the runaway note on her pillow and then the ransom note in the fold of the comforter."

"According to Ashley and Nadine," I say.

"Yeah. Ashley said she found the runaway note on her pillow that morning and Nadine said she found the ransom note in the comforter when she was making up the bed."

"Sounds like she didn't get very far in making up the bed," I say.

He shakes his head. "Not at all. I assumed she saw the note and just dropped the covers, but I shouldn't be assuming anything, should I?"

"We all do it," I say. "That's why it's so helpful to talk it through and ask and answer questions."

He nods, licks the last of the cobbler from his fork, and replaces the lid.

"So," I say, "the dog alerts on the bed . . ."

"And I think of course because the little girl slept there, spent more time there than any other single place. But then I realize . . . the dog isn't alerting on the bed so much as under the bed. And I start asking myself did I look under the bed earlier and . . . I know I did, I had to. There's no way I wouldn't look under her bed while searching the house, but in that moment I couldn't remember for sure and started doubting myself. Ronnie turns to me and says, 'She's under that bed. I'd bet $250,000.00.' And I'm .

.. just . . . I'm about to tell him to clear the room, take the dog out, and I'd lift the comforter with my gloved hands and look again, this time with a flashlight . . . but before I can do any of that Trace rushes in, slings back the covers, drops to his knees, and pulls the bound body of his lifeless little girl out from beneath the bed."

10

L ater that afternoon, as I'm driving home from the prison, I get a call from Randa Raffield's father, Jerry.

In addition to being an investigator at the Gulf County Sheriff's Department, I'm a part-time prison chaplain at Gulf Correctional Institution, and I had an afternoon shift of conducting crisis counseling, facilitating support groups, and attending meetings.

Though being an investigator with the sheriff's department gives me plenty to do, I enjoy being a prison chaplain and can't let it go. Each job is fulfilling and rewarding in a way the other is not, and I'm grateful I have the opportunity to do both.

"John?" Jerry says. "Can't believe I got you."

He has called several times since Daniel's return, but this is the first one I answered.

"I've been away," I say. "Sorry."

"I heard you got married. Congratulations."

Jerry Raffield, a psychologist living in Seaside, has stayed in touch with me since I first interviewed him about his missing daughter. Though she had vanished and cut off all communication with him, with everyone, he has expressed nothing but love for her and a desire to find her and be in her life again.

"I'm sure you know why I'm calling," he says.

"I bet I can guess," I say, "but why don't you tell me."

"I heard Randa returned Daniel safe and sound," he says.

"We got Daniel back," I say. "It's not entirely clear how."

"Surely she—"

"I think she drugged him the entire time she had him," I say.

"I truly believe she returned him," he says. "Unharmed. I take her at her word that she only took him for a little insurance. Think about what all she's been through. I'm sure she was just trying to protect herself."

"I can understand why you'd like to interpret all her actions in as favorable light as possible, but—"

"I'm aware of what I'm doing," he says. "I just feel so bad for her and what she's been through and I feel so guilty for not being there for her. She's my little girl and somehow I let her down."

"I understand," I say. "I do."

"I haven't given up on finding her and getting her the help she needs," he says. "I don't think she's beyond saving."

I don't want to believe anyone is beyond saving, but if Randa is a sociopath or has a borderline personality disorder, which I suspect is at least possible, then what she needs saving from more than anything else is herself.

"Has Daniel said anything that might help us find her?" he asks.

"He really doesn't remember much of anything at all," I say. "Maybe in time, but . . . I think it's doubtful."

"Has she been in contact with you anymore?" he says.

For a while, Randa was calling me quite often, but I haven't heard from her in a while now.

"Not lately, no," I say.

"Will you please let me know if she does or if Daniel remembers anything that might help us?" he says. "Please help me find my little girl and get her home safely."

If we ever find her, something we have so far not even come close to, I imagine her *home* will be prison or a mental institution. Not sure that's the *home* he means.

"I'll do my best," I say, and I mean it.

11

That night after we've put the girls to bed, Anna, Sam, Daniel, and I watch Trace Evers' music video for the song about and featuring Mariah.

The song is called *Never Leave You Again* and opens on a scene with Trace in prison and Mariah coming to visit. The two are separated by glass in a metal visiting booth and talk to each other on old fashion phone receivers.

"I miss you, Daddy," Mariah says into the phone as she holds her little hand up to the glass.

She's not only a truly beautiful photogenic little girl, but a natural entertainer, her performance relaxed and natural.

"I can't believe that energetic little beauty is dead," Anna says.

"I . . . want to . . . help . . . you burn . . . the . . . fucker . . . who . . . did it," Sam says from her hospital bed.

"I'm counting on all three of you to help," I say.

Without taking his eyes off the screen, Daniel nods. "Count on it."

"You know I'll always be your Watson," Anna says. "Or your huckleberry or whatever you want me to be."

While in the midst of an intensely emotional scene that has

Trace apologizing to Mariah, guards come and drag him away, his hand yanked away from the glass, leaving only her little hand on the glass as she yells, "No, Daddy, don't leave me. Daddy. Daddy. Daddy. Don't leave me."

The music, which is mostly a beat, then comes up and by the time Trace starts to rap, he's walking out of prison, Mariah running toward him from where she had been waiting with an older woman I believe we're meant to think is Trace's mother.

"I will never leave you again," Trace raps to a slow beat as Mariah jumps into his arms. "No, not ever. No, no matter what. I will never leave you again. My girl, my girl, my little girl."

After their tearful reunion, the two, father and daughter, take a tour of Atlanta together—zip-lining and rock climbing at SunTrust Park, eating cheeseburgers at the Varsity, climbing Stone Mountain.

"You, you are my life," Trace sings. "My reason for rapping, my reason for everything."

He sings from the empty stage at Chastain Park Amphitheater, her an audience of one with the best seat in the house.

They tour the MLK Center and the Georgia Aquarium and eat giant pieces of chocolate cake at the Landmark Diner.

"The old me is dead and gone. You got me rapping a brand new song."

In quick succession, shots of them at CNN, The World of Coca-Cola, The Fox, Underground, Piedmont Park fill the screen.

"I'm sorry for the pain I've caused. But that's over and done with now. You will never hurt again. I will never let you down. I will never leave you again. No not ever. No, no matter what."

When the video has concluded we all sit in silence for a few moments.

Eventually I say, "Some of the lines from the song are referenced in the ransom note."

"In . . . ter . . . esting," Sam says.

"He seems to really love and adore her," Anna says. "Not a lot of rappers with the image he portrays would write a song about their daughter and make a video of it."

I nod. I don't know much about rap music and rarely listen to it, but I recall a hit Eminem song from maybe a decade ago being about his daughter.

"Doesn't mean he didn't kill her," Daniel says.

"No it doesn't," Anna agrees.

"It had quite a few views before the murder," I say, "but since then it's shot up by six million."

"The visibility and media coverage of this case is staggering," Anna says.

"And it's just starting," Daniel adds.

As if to punctuate their points, when I exit out of YouTube and the TV returns to the cable feed, a news-as-entertainment talk show panel is discussing Mariah's case.

In the brief moments before I am able to turn it off all I hear from the so-called experts are self-serving statements and irresponsible speculation.

"You don't want to hear what they have to say?" Daniel asks.

I shake my head. "Not yet. Not sure if I ever will, but if there comes a time when I feel like I need to know what the public is hearing, I want to know far more of the facts than I do now. And at the moment it'd be hard to imagine knowing less."

12

W ith Anna asleep beside me, I strain to read the murder book by the narrow, pale light of a battery powered reading lamp on a clip.

The base of the small light is clipped to the front cover of the binder, the flexible arm bending down to position the lamp just above the area I'm trying to read, but the binder is too big and bulky to be reading in bed and the book light is too small, its illumination too weak to make this entire exercise anything but frustrating.

Next to me, Anna's constant, rhythmic breathing is reassuring, her warm, bare leg touching mine both comforting and arousing.

Both the fan and window unit are on low so the baby monitor, which is turned up to almost max volume, can be easily heard. Every breath and stir, toss and turn, of both girls is amplified, exaggerated, and I'm grateful for every decibel.

Having Johanna here on the weekends during the school year is nice, but frustrating in its brevity. Having her here with us nearly all the time for nearly all the summer is heaven.

Beside me on the nightstand are both of the weapons I wear

each day, but with Chris in town, acting the way he is, posing the potential threats he does, it's nice to have Daniel, who is also armed, sleeping in the living room.

Daniel, the retired college professor who suffers from panic attacks and has never carried a weapon in his life, has said since his return from wherever Randa Raffield had him that he will never be unarmed anywhere anytime again.

All of this recedes a bit as I read the murder book and am transported back into Mariah's rented bedroom as her body is discovered.

When Trace reaches under the bed and pulls out the broken body of the greatest love in his life he begins to wail in ways Arnie has never heard.

And even as evidence is being contaminated and destroyed, Arnie finds it nearly impossible to tell the young anguished father to place the body of his daughter on the floor and leave the room.

Behind him the K-9 dog is yelping and Ronnie Wyrick is saying something he can't make out.

Eventually, Ronnie orders the dog out and helps Arnie coax Mariah's body out of Trace's arms and Trace out of the room.

Suddenly alone with the body, Arnie gets his first unimpeded glance at the unimaginable horror of what's before him.

Only partially visible because of the fleece throw she's wrapped in, Mariah's body tells two different tales. A glance at her flawless young face and she appears to be sleeping, but the black ropes coiling around her cold skin and connecting her wrists and ankles like deadly serpents attempting to consume each other contradict what that first glance seems to say.

Part of the reason she appears to be asleep is there are no visible signs of violence, no obvious trauma or clear cause of death.

Wake up, he wants to tell her. *Please just wake up.*

But he knows with the certainty of skin that is cold to the

touch that this exquisite, innocent child will never wake again in this life.

"John," Anna whispers. "John."

I open my eyes to see her hovering over me.

"What's wrong?" I say, pushing myself up.

When the bed is harder than it's supposed to be and doesn't give when I push up on it, I realize I'm not in our bed at all, but on the floor in the girls' room.

The nightlight gives the small room a nice warm glow and Johanna and Taylor's breathing sounds like the sweetest music I've ever heard.

"Nothing," she says. "I woke and you weren't in bed."

"Came in here to be close to them and must have fallen asleep."

She nods and gives me a smile and a kiss on the head.

"Lay back down," she says. "I'll be right back."

I do as I'm told and in a few moments she returns with our pillows and a blanket and joins me on the floor between our children.

"Not that they'll let us sleep that long, but I brought your phone so you'll have your alarm," she says.

"You're the best wife in the world," I say.

"Did you come in here because of what you were reading?" she asks.

I nod. "And thinking. And it's not just Mariah. Brings back Nicole Caldwell, Martin Fisher, LaMarcus Williams, Cedric Porter . . . so many . . . so much."

She pulls me into her arms and the warmth of her body and the kindness of her concern vanquishes all thoughts of the vulnerable and victimized, and soon I am drifting back into sweet oblivion surrounded by my three favorite girls in the world.

13

The next morning, Arnie, Keisha, Jessica, and I meet with Reggie in her office to go over the FDLE crime scene collection log.

After FDLE processes the crime scene, they send us an inventory of what evidence they collected and we have to determine what to test and how.

Jessica Young is our department's non-sworn crime scene tech. Keisha Colvin is the FDLE agent assigned to assist in the investigation.

It's Reggie's first day back and she's still moving quite gingerly.

"Okay," she says, looking at her copy of the list we all have, "let's figure this out as fast as we can so we can get moving on this. Lot of people are waiting for these results and it seems like the whole world is watching."

Because of limited time and resources and because certain types of testing exclude others, we've got to let the FDLE lab know what we want done with each item they collected—even if what we want done is nothing at all.

"Let's start with the biggest nightmare," she says. "Fingerprints."

"It's a rental," Arnie says, "and there are a lot of prints, but not as many as you'd think."

"I'm assuming it's cleaned pretty well between guests," Reggie says.

"It is," he says, "and that's our saving grace."

"We've printed the cleaning lady," Keisha says, "and the family, workers, friends, and neighbors who we know went into the house. We're also trying to track down the past few guests before Mariah's family to print them for exclusion too."

Keisha Colvin is a stout and powerful forty-something African-American woman with dark skin and shortish hair that appears to have a will of its own.

"Once we've finished with all that," Arnie says, "we're going to be down to a pretty reasonable amount of unknown prints to deal with."

"Most important objects to check prints for are those that came into the house with family," Jessica says. "We know no previous guests' prints should be on those."

"True."

"And of course anything used in the commission of the crime," she says. "The ropes, the blanket, whatever the weapon is determined to be."

"We meet with the medical examiner tomorrow," Reggie says. "Get the preliminary autopsy results back. Maybe we'll find out cause of death and figure out what was used."

"Hope so," Arnie says.

"Okay," Reggie says, "let's work our way through the list of what was collected. All the bedding from Mariah's bed. Assuming we want DNA testing on all of it and the blanket Mariah was wrapped in and the pajamas she was wearing."

Jessica nods and says, "Touch DNA tests too, right?"

Everyone agrees.

Certain tests conflict with each other and can't both be done, so part of what we're doing is assigning priority. If touch DNA *and* fingerprinting or some other test can't both be done, we're going with touch DNA.

Keisha says, "The lab has identified what they believe could be semen smears on the bedsheets, along with a pubic hair."

"That could be huge," Arnie says. "It's something like that that's going to help us get a conviction."

"I see the clothes on the floor and the sheets, pillow cases, and blankets from the bunk beds as low priorities," Reggie says. "Whatta y'all think?"

We all agreed.

The clothes Trace was wearing when he pulled Mariah out from beneath the bed and held her were also collected, and we all agreed they needed to be checked for hair and fibers and DNA.

"Everyone agree the ropes used to tie the vic—to tie Mariah up, should have extremely high priority for DNA testing?" Reggie says.

Everyone agrees.

"I think we need handwriting analysis and fingerprinting done on both notes," Reggie says.

"We've collected handwriting samples from everyone who was in the house that night," Keisha says. "We also took some of Mariah's writing samples from a notebook with her things and her dad's songwriting journal that she doodled in sometimes too."

"She actually wrote some lyrics in both notebooks," Arnie says. "Wanted to be a songwriter like her dad. So we should have plenty to use for comparison."

"As the investigation widens and we speak to more and more people," Reggie says, "I want handwriting samples and finger-prints from everyone and I want to know anyone who refuses."

"Will do," Arnie says.

"What about the zip ties?" Reggie asks. "If we can't do both, and I'm pretty sure we can't, fingerprint or DNA?"

Even though rope was used to tie Mariah up, three zip ties were found at the scene—one in her bedroom, one on the stairs, and one on the porch.

Checking them for fingerprints is the consensus.

"Glove," Reggie says. "Same question."

A single aqua latex glove had also been found at the scene—in the bathroom connected to Mariah's bedroom. According to statements by Trace, Ashley, Nadine, and Irvin, the glove wasn't there the night before and didn't belong to anyone in the house.

"Definitely DNA," Jessica says.

"And the metal pieces?"

Two tiny metal pieces—one flat, the other cylindrical—were discovered on the floor near the door inside Mariah's room. Above them on the wall was a scuff mark and indentation in the sheetrock Nadine said was not there the night before when she put Mariah to bed.

"Prints," Jessica says.

Everyone seems to be in agreement.

"Okay," Reggie says, "Let give the lab a call and cover this and see what kind of time we're looking at."

She calls the lab and puts the tech on speaker.

As she goes over the list, it becomes increasingly obvious that much of the testing is going to take far longer than we would like.

"You caught any of the news lately?" Reggie says. "This is the highest profile murder case in the country right now. We're under tremendous pressure to clear it, to get results . . . like yesterday. Isn't there anything you can do to help us get the results back any faster?"

"We'll do what we can," the tech says, "but it won't be much faster no matter what we do. Especially the DNA. Might want to use a different lab for it—or at least some of it."

The services FDLE provides for smaller departments like

ours costs our department nothing. The crime scene investigation that was done, the lab work that will be done, the agent provided, in this case Keisha Colvin, is absolutely free. If Reggie wants another lab—either an independent one or one belonging to a larger county such as Broward, Dade, or Hillsborough—she will have to pay for it out of her limited department budget. Unless, as is sometimes the case, the sheriff of a larger department with a dedicated lab insists on running the tests as a favor because it has no budgetary impact on his or her department.

"I'll call around and see what I can find out," Reggie says.

If Reggie finds another lab to run the tests sooner, the FDLE lab will box up the evidence being transferred and ship it via FedEx so that when it's signed for, chain of custody can be maintained.

It takes several calls and a fair amount of logistics, but Reggie finally finds a couple of labs that can do the test sooner and that we can afford. FDLE will be taking care of the fingerprints and certain other tests while a lab in Tampa and one in Miami will take care of the others.

"It's the best result we're going to get," Reggie says, "and though it's going to be relatively fast, the case will already be long since concluded in the court of public opinion before we get a single result back."

14

Later that afternoon, Reggie and I drive out to the Cape together to do a walkthrough of the crime scene before the yellow tape comes down and the rental company starts to clean it in preparation for future rentals—which I'm told will quadruple because of true crime tourists alone.

Cape San Blas is situated on a peninsula that begins just a few miles from the town of Port St. Joe. It's a small but popular beach vacation destination made up of homes and cottages instead of condos, surrounded by woodlands and pristine beaches instead of tourist attractions and amusements.

Unlike Panama City Beach or Daytona, older wealthy couples and younger wealthy families come to the quiet, rustic, isolated strip of snow white and sugar fine sand.

St. Joseph's Peninsula is a narrow finger of land some ten miles long with the Gulf of Mexico on one side and St. Joseph Bay on the other. At its westernmost point is a state park popular among campers, hikers, swimmers, fishers, kayakers, and bird-watchers.

We drive out on 30A, the rustic road lined with pines and

palms, passing more media vans than tourists as we do. I'm driving and Reggie, who probably shouldn't be back at work yet, is sitting at an odd angle in the passenger seat, attempting to sit without putting pressure on the worst of her wounds.

"You listened to or read the transcripts of the interviews with Trace and the others yet?" Reggie asks.

"Plan to tonight," I say.

"When the ME concludes the autopsy and releases the body, they plan to return to Atlanta for the funeral," she says. "I'd like you to interview them before that happens."

I nod.

"Which means it will probably have to be tomorrow."

"Okay."

"They're cooperating and have said they'll come back when we need them to, but . . . that doesn't mean they really will."

"Be much more challenging if we have to coordinate and conduct interviews in Atlanta," I say. "Let alone make an arrest."

"Fulton County Sheriff's office will help, but you're right. Won't be easy."

The first part of 30A looks as rural as any other road in Gulf County, tall pines rising above the highway on both sides, their backlit bases striping the blacktop, their tops dappling the grassy shoulders beyond.

"You got any thoughts on this yet?" she asks.

"None worth sharing," I say.

"It's early, I know, but . . ."

"We'll know far more in another day or so," I say. "Seeing the house will help. Reading the interviews—conducting some ourselves. Going over the crime scene photos. And especially . . . getting the results of the autopsy. Without knowing cause of death it's impossible to even theorize—and of course we don't need to do too much of that until we get the lab results back. Be setting ourselves up for disaster to form many opinions until we get the fingerprints, handwriting samples, and DNA results back."

"I've never felt this far behind this early in a case before," she says. "I tell you the governor called this morning?"

I shake my head.

"And it wasn't for the reason he claimed—expressing support and pledging resources. It was to remind me how high profile this thing is and to get it right but do it fast."

Suddenly the dense pine forest to our right gives way to a low-lying pine prairie where young, narrow trees with a lot of space between them are scattered about, beyond them the bay and beyond the bay more pines on the peninsula curving away from us westwardly.

"Made me glad I blew my budget and hired the outside labs to do some of the testing so we get the results back quicker," she says.

I nod. "Maybe we'll get lucky and some of the sheriffs won't charge us for the work their labs do."

"To be honest with you, that's what I'm counting on," she says. "The private labs, which will absolutely charge us, are going to break the bank as it is."

"Sorry," I say, and am thankful again that I never have to deal with budgets or administrative issues. They affect the work I do, of course, but nothing I do affects them, which is freeing.

"Someone said Merrill is working for the defense team," she says.

I nod. "That's what I hear."

"You haven't spoken with him about it yet?"

"Not yet."

"Is it going to be a problem?"

I shake my head.

"You sure?"

"Positive."

"Wish I could say the same for me and Merrick."

"I just mean no matter what happens or how this all plays out Merrill and I will still be friends."

"Wish I could say the same for me and Merrick."

15

After pulling through the gate at the entrance of Stars Haven where several news crews are still stationed, we drive back to the pale blue beach house mansion that still has yellow crime scene tape flapping around the bottom of it.

Built up on stilts, the ground level is a six-car garage, the platform for the elevated pool, and the housing for the elevator shaft. The crime scene tape is wrapped around the stilts and is whipped around violently in the beach breeze blowing in off the Gulf.

Beyond the massive pastel monstrosity, a private boardwalk extends out between sand dunes and sea oats down to the beach.

The three livable levels are some 10,000 square feet, with an elevated pool and deck on the first story, seven bedrooms, nine bathrooms, an elevator, a gym, and three wet bars.

Inside, the enormous rooms are plush and opulent and alternate between beach *chic* and Gulfside gaudy, and it has the feel of someone's beachfront mansion far more than rental property. Which it is. This obscene monument to selfishness and hubris was designed and built by the insurance magnate and real estate developer Roger Garrett. In fact, Garrett developed the entire Stars Haven community but only owns this home.

"Place rents for three thousand a week," Reggie says, as we stand in the open concept first story with a view of the sprawling kitchen, dining room, breakfast nook, wet bar area, and living room.

The living room alone is large enough for two full sectionals, a giant fireplace, and the biggest TV I've ever seen.

"How often you think that fireplace gets used?" she asks.

"Probably far more than it should," I say. "I hear a lot of tourists crank the AC way up and build big fires."

"You could build a bonfire in that bitch," she says.

We look around some more.

"It's no wonder someone had the idea for a kidnap-ransom," she says. "Wonder why he asked for such a relatively small amount?"

"We figure that out and we'll be well on our way to catching him," I say.

"'Course there may not have been an attempted kidnaping at all," she says. "This level is the only realistic entrance to the house—that's two doors, front and back—and the family claims they were locked. They were locked when they went to bed and they were locked when they got up the next morning. And there were no signs of a break-in."

"But they didn't set the alarm," I say. "And it's a rental. No telling how many keys to this place are floating around out there. The owners have keys—and no telling how many of their family and friends. The rental agents have keys. The cleaning service. And anyone who has rented it in the past could've made copies of the keys."

"All true," she says, "but what's more likely? That? Or someone in the house did it?"

"Of course," I say. "I'm just trying to think through all possibilities."

I step over to the huge sliding glass door in the back, looking past a large bronze sea turtle on one side and a brightly painted dolphin on a stand on the other to the deck and bar and pool beyond.

"I realize there are the only two main doors on this floor—this one and the front one, but each level has a balcony and french doors that lead out."

"Sure," she says, "a world class gymnast could shimmy up the balcony and break in, but one set of french doors open into the master suite with Trace and Ashley in it and the other opens into the nanny's room."

"Didn't say it was likely, just possible."

"But is it really?"

I nod. "Possible. Not probable."

She steps over and joins me at the back door. "Bet you that bronze sea turtle and funky colored dolphin costs more than we make in a month."

Beyond the pool and deck a set of wooden stairs leads down to a boardwalk that leads down to the beach. Above the beach and the green Gulf rolling in and returning from it, the clouded ceiling of sky blushes with the reflection of the late-afternoon sun.

"There were a lot of people in here the night before the murder," she says. "Trace threw some sort of celebration party for his record going platinum. Plus the event was live on Facebook so no telling how many head cases and pedos saw it."

"Someone could have come to the party and stayed in the house," I say. "It's big enough. Could've hidden and waited for an opportune time. How many people at the party?"

"Not sure. More than fifty, less than a hundred."

"These people who drove down from Atlanta or—"

"Some, yeah. Others were some of Ashley's old friends from the area and her family."

"None of them crashed here after the party?"

"Not according to the statements given by the family."

"What'd they do on the Fourth?"

"Was just family, the nanny, and the manager," she says. "Went into town to watch fireworks."

"Someone could've gotten in then," I say. "While they were in town."

"Sure. They came back home and did a few of their own down on the beach. Everyone was tired. Crashed when they came in. Early night according to them."

"Who put the kids to bed?" I ask.

"The nanny. Says Brett was still up playing a video game in his room when she went to bed, but Mariah was out like a light."

We cross the room and climb the stairs, pausing at the landing on the second floor, before continuing to Mariah's room.

"She was isolated from the parents up here," I say, "but Brett and Nadine were on either side of her. You'd think one of them would've heard if there had been any screams or loud noises."

Because the rooms are large, there is more space between them than normal, but the doors to them are within twenty feet of each other.

"Yeah. They say they didn't, but I'm looking forward to re-interviewing all of them."

"Me too."

We stand at the door to the kids' room where the notes and Mariah were found.

With the beds stripped and other items collected as evidence missing and the white walls and furniture still smudged with black fingerprinting powder and the evidence markers still scattered about and sections of carpet removed, the room is an incongruous contradiction of festive beachy pastel colors surrounded by white walls and bright multicolored carpet contrasted with the harsh, industrial, blunt, dirty, damaging remnants and reminders of a processed crime scene.

Mariah's full-size bed is centered along the far wall in, the long side against the wall. To the left of it is a bright aqua-colored couch with a white pillow with bold pink letters on it that read Don't Worry! Be Happy! To the right of her bed, along the right wall is a set of white wooden bunkbeds, a white ladder extending at an angle down to the floor. Two smallish windows, their blinds pulled up, look out onto the side yard and the next house, which though huge, is small compared to this one. Scattered throughout the room are a few nightstands, a dresser, a chest of drawers, a large wardrobe, a desk with some crayons, colored pencils, construction paper, and a partially open stapler, and a huge TV mounted to the wall. The other walls are decorated with beach, sea, and nautical items—all painted in a clash of bright primary and pastel colors. In the front left corner is a private bathroom.

We look through the room and bathroom, slowly, carefully, methodically, though we're not here to collect evidence or spot something that might have been missed. The excellent FDLE crime scene team didn't miss anything. We are here for our own benefit, to take a firsthand look at the house, see what crime scene photos can't show us, get familiar with the area we'll be talking about during the investigation and hopefully the court proceedings.

We then take a tour through the room Nadine was staying in. Followed by the room at the opposite end that Brett was staying in.

After we had seen everything there was to see on this level, we conducted a few tests. With all bedroom doors closed, Reggie stood in Mariah's room and yelled and screamed while I listened from Nadine's and then Brett's. Though muffled and relatively low, I could hear her from both rooms.

We then walk through the other levels much more quickly and finish just as Ashley's ex arrives.

16

"Am I a suspect?" Justin Harris asks.

We are standing in the enormous, open kitchen of the beachfront mansion where we've just asked him for his fingerprints and a writing sample.

"Are you refusing?" Reggie asks.

"No," he says shaking his head. "Not at all. I'm just curious. I guess I would be—a suspect that is—I just . . . it's just funny. I don't know. I'm happy to help. I'm here to cooperate. I just thought I was here to answer questions about the house and share some things with you I think you need to know."

"Write this please," Reggie says, placing a sheet of paper with certain words on it beside the blank notebook paper and pen already on the marble top of the island.

"Sure," he says. "No problem."

Justin Harris is a mid-thirties man in navy work slacks, cheap dress shoes, and a white sports shirt with his name and the name of his rental company embroidered on it.

He presents as a man with an IQ on the low end of average who is working very hard to run the company he inherited from his father but struggling to do so.

"Can you talk while you do that?" Reggie asks.

The rhythm and strategy we had developed since we began working together is for her to take the lead and ask most of the early questions, allowing me to observe how the person responds and have time to think.

"Sure," he says.

"Tell me about your relationship with Ashley," she says.

"We were kids. Well, she was. I was, mentally. I was from down here. She was from Wewa. We met at a party. I was older. She was smoking hot. She was a teen mom, but that wasn't something she told me 'til later—after I had fallen for her."

As he talks, he continues to copy the words and sentences from the sample Reggie placed on the countertop. Without seeming to realize what he's doing, he occasionally writes some of the words he's saying along with the ones he's copying.

"Between us . . . I think Ashley feels kinda bad for me," he says. "Probably why they vacationed here. Knew I could use the commission."

"Why would she feel bad for you?"

"Like guilty I mean," he says. "My family had money. She was very poor. She pursued me. I think she was trying to find security and a father for her baby. She never said anything like that, and she wasn't bad to me while we were together, but . . . the moment something better came along . . . she was gone."

"You said your family had money," Reggie says. "Not anymore?"

"It's a tough market right now," he says.

The truth is there's nothing wrong with the market. It's the manager. The agency did extremely well when his dad ran it, but since his dad's death and the company becoming his, everything except the market is down—rentals, income, valuation.

"So you need money?"

Obviously the family knows about the ransom note, but we've been able to keep it from going public. I wonder if he knows about it. Did Ashley tell him? Had they spoken since it happened?

He stops writing and looks up at her. "Everybody needs money, but I'm not like destitute or anything. I just think she . . . It's her way of paying me back. I was good to her. And to Brett."

He answers as if he doesn't know about the ransom note.

"I don't know if you suspect her or not," he says. "Hell, if you suspect me, you must suspect everybody. But there's no way she could kill anyone. And especially not a child. And that fact that she's trying to pay me back for the help I gave her when she needed it shows what a decent person she is."

He finishes the writing sample and drops the pen on it.

"Now we need to get you printed," Reggie says.

"My prints will be all over this place," he says. "This is one of my listings. I'm in here all the time."

"That's why we need them," she says. "To exclude you."

"Oh. Sure. Okay."

As she rolls his fingers across the small portable digital reader, he says, "I still can't believe what happened. What did happen exactly?"

"You don't know?" I say.

"Just what's online, but . . . that's not much. Suspicious death, but no details."

"You haven't spoken to Ashely since it happened?" I ask.

"Called and left a message for her, told her how sorry I was and to let me know if I could do anything, but I haven't heard back from her yet."

"We haven't released any information like that to the public yet," Reggie says.

What she doesn't say is that we don't yet have that informa-tion—and won't until we hear back from the ME.

"How many sets of keys are there to this property?" I ask. "And who all has them?"

He shrugs. "I'm not sure exactly. I can try to find out, but . . .

the owner, Roger Garrett, has a few sets I'm sure. We have three sets I think. I can look when I get back to the office. Did the killer use a key to get in?"

"Killer?" Reggie says. "How'd you get from *suspicious death* to *killer*?"

"Because of all this," he says, nodding to her printing him. "And all the questions. And crime scene tape. And there are plenty of rumors flying around out there—locally, like here on the street, and on TV and the internet."

"Are any of the sets of keys or individual keys you have missing?" I ask.

"Not that I know of, but . . . nothing like this has ever happened before. I . . . We've never had any problems or issues before. I'll have to double check, but . . . I don't think so. I just don't know."

"What about—how do the maids get into clean?" Reggie says.

"They come by the office and get their assignments and keys. I gave Arnie a list of our cleaners and recent guests."

Reggie finishes printing him and he thanks her, which sounds odd.

"Don't know why I said that," he says. "Sorry."

"Is there a hidden key anywhere on the property?" I ask.

When I say *hidden* he begins to nod, but by the time I get to the end of the sentence he's shaking his head.

"No," he says. "Not that I know of."

"Why did you nod at first?" I ask. "What did you think I was asking? What else is hidden here?"

"The room," he says. "I thought you meant the hidden room."

17

"Looks like we won't be releasing this property back to you today after all," Reggie says.

"Really?" Justin asks. "Why?"

We are standing just above and outside the hidden room.

"Is that an actual question?" she says. "Because we have to have the crime scene techs process it."

"Oh. Really? But if no one knew it was there and didn't have a key to get in it . . ."

"We can't know that for sure, can we?"

"Guess not. Sorry. But I really don't think anyone knows about it but me and the owner."

For what reason exactly I'm not sure, but the homeowner had a hidden room constructed in the house. It's located in the bottom of the elevator shaft and is accessed by raising the false floor once the elevator has left the first level.

According to Justin, only two keys to this room exist. One is kept in the owner's possession, the other stays locked in the safe at his office—except for days like today when he gets it out and brings it with him to the house.

With gloved hands, we take the key from him and follow his

instructions on raising the elevator and lifting the false floor to reveal the locked door beneath.

"See?" he says. "No way anyone even knew about this, let alone got in it."

"Tell you what," Reggie says. "We're gonna keep your key. You go back to your office and double check on the other sets of keys for us. We're gonna process this room. When we're finished— unless there are any other surprises you want to tell us about— we'll bring your key to you and release the property."

"No, no other surprises. Sorry about this one. I really didn't think of it. Most owners who rent have a locked room they keep their personal things in."

"Sure," she says, "but not a hidden safe room in an elevator shaft."

Twenty minutes later, with Justin gone and Jessica joining us, we enter Roger Garrett's secret room.

Reggie has decided to let Jessica process the room instead of calling FDLE back in, but if we encounter anything that warrants calling them, we'll ease out and do just that.

Jessica has already dusted the false floor and door for prints and is now suited up and leading the way.

The steel door is heavy but on a hydraulic system that makes it easy to lift. As it comes up, soft lights around the room come on.

Beneath it, a set of metal stairs leads down into the room.

Though tall, the room is no wider than an elevator shaft. It sits on the ground floor in the center of the six-car garage, which from the outside just appears to be the enclosed shaft of the elevator.

The hidden room is essentially a bomb shelter or safe room with reinforced steel walls and its own air filtration system and power supply.

Apart from the paranoia and fear for a bleak future, the

saddest thing about the room by far is it's designed for one person—presumably Roger Garrett. A lone recliner sits in the center of the room surrounded by survival supplies, weapons, and communications devices.

"Can y'all see any sign that anyone's been in here recently?" she says.

"Hard to tell," Jessica says.

"Well, John and I will clear out of here and let you process it. Let me know if you find anything. Looks like ol' Roger plans to ride out the apocalypse right here."

"Or a hurricane or home invasion," I say. "He's equally set for all."

18

That evening I met Merrill at the old gym to play basketball.

What everyone refers to as the *old gym* is a freestanding red brick gymnasium on Main Street that was once part of the elementary school. When the school was torn down, a few classrooms left on one end of the property were restored and remodeled and became part of a pre-school and across the now-empty field, where once stood the main body of the school, is the old gym.

Merrill is part of an area league team that practices here and has a key to this huge old building that looks and smells the same as it did decades ago.

I grew up loving basketball, but stopped playing after what happened to Martin Fisher in Atlanta.

After several years of not playing, I was playing again, and Merrill and I, who were on the high school team together, are playing more one-on-one these days than jogging or anything else.

Since high school, I had played mostly on outdoor asphalt courts, which presented challenges—such as heat, light, rain, wind—that having access to our own gym does not.

We sit lacing them up on the old wooden bleachers we had as kids when the Pottersville Elementary team played Wewa Elementary in after school afternoon matchups.

"We straight?" Merrill says.

It's just the two of us in the enormous old gym and his words seem to get lost in all the open space.

"Always," I say.

"Sorry I had to call in the second string to look out for Sam and Daniel," he says.

I smile. "Not sure Dad and Verna see themselves as the second string, but it's no problem."

"It was only for the last day."

"Wouldn't matter if it had been for more. It's all good."

"How about me working Trace?" he asks. "You got a problem with that?"

I shake my head. "Wouldn't matter if I did," I say, "but I don't."

"Told him I'll follow where the case takes me no matter where that is. He said that's what he wants me to do because it won't lead me back to him 'cause he didn't do it. Said what he wants most in this world if he can't have his little girl back is to find the fucker that took her from him."

I nod.

"Thing is . . . you weren't here," he says. "Couldn't count on the investigation going like it should from the beginning—most important time."

I continue to nod, not pointing out that I can screw up the early hours of an investigation with the best of them.

"I want whoever did this," he says. "Don't care who it is. Knew takin' the job would give me access nobody else would have."

He's right. He does have access I'll never get, and it could prove to be extremely useful.

"Not that I'm working for you or the po-lice or anyone else. I really don't think he did it, but . . . it comes to it, I'll be in a position to know shit and do shit."

I would've thought it went without saying that he wasn't working for me or law enforcement, but I would have been wrong.

"And I didn't want this ending up like Girl X," he says. "There was some attention at first, but I wondered how long it would last for the mixed girl of a mid-list rapper."

Just days after JonBenét's murder another young girl was savagely attacked in Chicago, but she didn't receive even a fraction of the attention that JonBenét did. The nine-year-old African-American girl, who became known as Girl X to protect her identity, was viciously assaulted, brutally raped, choked, tortured, had gang signs scrawled on her body and roach poison poured down her throat and left for dead in an apartment at Chicago's infamous Cabrini-Green public housing complex. It seems as if the entire world knows who JonBenét is, but nearly no one has ever heard the name Shatoya Currie, who survived her rape and attempted murder, but has brain damage, blindness, deafness, and is wheelchair bound.

"Trace is paying me," he says, "but I'm working for Mariah."

"Never doubted it."

"And if he did it, I'll help you burn him just as quick as anybody else."

19

The next morning we get the autopsy report back.

After reading and rereading it several times, there's still much I don't understand or know how to interpret.

Thankfully, the medical examiner has agreed to answer our questions.

Arnie, Keisha, Jessica, and I are with Reggie in her office. Dr. Luttrell is on speakerphone.

Raymond Luttrell is the medical examiner for the 14th Judicial Circuit, which covers Bay, Gulf, Calhoun, Holmes, Washington, and Jackson counties. He's calling us from his office in Panama City.

We don't take the time to go over the report line by line, which would be a waste of everybody's time. Instead, we ask him the questions most relevant to our investigation.

"Thank you again for doing this, Dr. Luttrell," Reggie says. "We really appreciate it. We know how busy you are and won't take up too much of your time. Let's start with the most pressing question for us—cause of death. Can you tell us what Mariah died from in the simplest terms?"

"Blunt force trauma," he says. "Quite simply a blow to the

head. A subdural hematoma. Her skull was fractured. It was an extremely violent blow."

"I saw her head at the crime scene when the body was first discovered," Arnie says. "It looked fine. No blood. No marks. Nothing."

"What little there was to see was hidden by her hair," Luttrell says. "But there wasn't much to see. Remember the skin is elastic. When the blow happened, the skin stretched inward and then out again. There was a very small laceration, but not much blood. Death occurred quite quickly so the heart was no longer pumping the blood out of the small scalp laceration."

"Any indication of the weapon used?" Reggie asks.

Parents who kill their kids typically use what is known as a *personal weapon* to either beat, choke, or drown them—particularly in cases involving underage children. I can't help but believe that if we discover the weapon used on Mariah, we'll stand a much, much better chance of identifying her killer.

"I'm afraid I can be of no assistance there," he says. "There's nothing to indicate what it was. Though if you find it, there might be hair and traces of blood and cerebrospinal fluid. I wouldn't think there would be much, but even microscopic amounts can confirm it is the murder weapon."

Reggie starts to stay something, but he interrupts her.

"Sorry," he says, "I need to go back to something I said earlier. I described the blow as vicious, but that was more of an emotional reaction to it happening to a little girl. The truth is, a child that age, the skull is still quite thin. Sixteenth of an inch."

"So it wouldn't require a lot of strength to wield a weapon that would cause that kind of trauma," Jessica adds.

"Exactly," he says. "Quite right."

"What about the ropes," Reggie says, "Was she strangled or choked during the assault?"

"There's no evidence of strangulation," he says.

"So her restraints have nothing to do with her death," Reggie says, "apart from restraining her."

"I can't be certain they even did that," he says. "Normally I'd expect to see some bruising and abrasions on the skin beneath and around the restraints—at least the wrists, ankles, and neck where the victim moved or struggled against the restraints. It's not always the case, but more often than not there would be bruising and abrading. In this case we have neither. Which could mean nothing, but if it does mean something, I can think of three possible explanations for their absence. The victim was willingly restrained—or at least didn't struggle against the restraints, possibly due to some sort of threat or coercion. To me, this is the least likely scenario, but is at least possible. The other two are far more likely in my opinion. The victim could have been tied up postmortem or died so soon after being bound that she didn't have time to struggle against the restraints."

I can think of at least one other possibility that would explain the forensic findings. There would be no bruising or abrading of the skin if Mariah was unconscious when tied up and killed. The thought of her being unconscious during her assault brings a certain comfort and I retroactively wish and pray for it to be so.

"How long before we get toxicology back?" I ask. "Is it possible there was no bruising and abrasions because she was unconscious?"

"Yes, that too is a possibility."

'Tis a consummation devoutly to be wish'd, I think.

"That would be a grace," Keisha says.

"Yes it would," Reggie says.

"I'm sorry to say I don't expect us to find that that was indeed the case," Luttrell says. "But we're looking at four to six weeks."

We are all quiet a beat as we let both of those bits of information sink in.

"What about time of death?" Arnie asks. "Anything you can tell us on that?"

"Just a range I'm afraid," Luttrell says. "My best guess is between ten the night of the fourth and six the morning of the fifth."

"Looking at your notations on livor mortis," I say, "is it safe to say that her body wasn't moved after lividity was set?"

"Yes, that's correct," he says. "The body could have been moved after death, but not after about six hours after death."

"Anything else?" Reggie asks.

No one says anything.

"I saved this one for last because I've been delaying it as long as possible," she says. "Was she sexually assaulted? The way I read the autopsy . . . she was, but . . ."

"To me that's the most fascinating finding," Luttrell says. "Given the way she was tied up—a way that can only be described as erotic bondage, I would've predicted we would find evidence of sexual trauma. And we did, but here's the strange thing. It didn't occur around the time of death, so it wasn't part of her being tied up the way she was or being killed. The vaginal trauma she suffered had already started to heal. I'd say it occurred approximately twenty-four to thirty-six hours prior to her death."

20

"Merrill says you're very good at this," Trace Evers says. "Says if anyone can figure out who did this, you can. Says I can trust you."

We—he, Merrill, Irvin Hunter and I—are on the screened-in back porch of a large home overlooking the Chipola River. The house is high, the backyard steep as it slopes down to the river below.

Hunter found this place online—at Airbnb or For Rent By Owner, or some such site—when Trace found that he couldn't stay with Ashley's family another moment.

"I trust Merrill," he says. "He says I can trust you, I trust you."

I haven't asked for his trust and probably won't really need it, though it can't hurt. What I need is his cooperation—which I'm hoping his trust will lead to.

"But . . . the news reports keep quoting unnamed sources close to the investigation saying I . . . that I . . . killed my own . . . little girl. Or if I didn't . . . someone else in the house that night. Y'all just lookin' at me, at us?"

I shake my head.

"Don't tell me you haven't heard them sayin' it over and over."

"I haven't," I say. "I haven't watched or read any of the coverage so far."

"For real?"

"I'm about as close to the investigation as you can get," I say, "and feel free to use my name. We are open to and looking at every possible suspect and every possible scenario. You have my word on that."

"Then tell me what you need to find whoever did this to my little girl," he says.

He pauses for a moment in what looks like an attempt to keep from breaking down, but then breaks down anyway, tears creasing his already red eyes and streaming down his cheeks.

"Still can't believe she's ..."

Trace "Evidence" Evers doesn't look, act, or sound like a successful rapper. He's dressed modestly in t-shirt and jeans. He's soft spoken and none of the words he's speaking sound street or ex-con, not angry, cocky, or defiant.

"She was my . . . little angel. My everything. She mattered more to me than anything in this world."

From across the porch, Irvin Hunter clears his throat and says, "And the whole world knew it. I'm tellin' you, somebody wanted to get to you ... they knew what to do."

Older than Trace and not half as polished, Hunter looks and sounds like what he is—a hanger-on. Trace feels like he owes him from their time in prison together and Hunter is taking full advantage.

Trace is shaking his head as he looks down. "If this is because of me ..."

I realize Trace is broken, brought low by the loss of his little girl, but I can tell by his manner and bearing and speech just how much of his public persona is just that—the affect of an entertainer in a certain medium and genre with its own conventions and expectations.

"If someone who I invited to my party, into my home . . ." Trace says.

"Let's start there," I say. "You're talking about the party you had here on the third, right? Who did the inviting? Did you know everyone who came?"

He nods. "There were a few faces I didn't recognize," he says. "Always are. Somebody brings somebody. Somebody crashes. But the whole thing was pretty chill. Not many people period and we included the kids for the first part of it."

"And after that?"

"We sort of split up the adults and the kids a little later that night."

"There were only a few kids," Hunter says. "No more than, what, five? And two of 'em were yours."

"Where'd they go?" I ask. "What'd they do?"

"Nanny took them upstairs to play," Trace says. "We stayed down—mostly out on the deck by the pool, but some people were inside, others on the beach."

"Truth is," Hunter adds, "people were all over the place, but she wasn't killed that night."

"And Nadine was watching the kids," Trace says. "The whole time."

I nod.

"I've made you a list of who was at the party that we know about," Trace says.

Hunter stands, crosses the porch, and hands me a sheet of paper with fifty or so names on it, then returns to his seat.

I glance at the list. Beside each name is an address or at least the name of a city and a word of identification—such as media or friend or publicist or rapper or actor or family.

"Don't get me wrong," Trace says. "I'm not trying to cast suspicion on anyone. But I want you looking at everyone. I know you're looking at me, at us, and I want you to. I just don't want you to focus on us so much that you don't find the real killer. I'm cooperating in every way I know how so you can clear us and move on to find the killer. So let me know what I can do —what we can do. We'll take a polygraph or whatever. Just tell me."

"Thank you," I say. "That will be very helpful for the investigation."

FDLE has a tech who administers polygraphs, but I'm far more inclined to use CVSA or computer voice stress analyzer on them—and we have an investigator in-house certified to run it.

"Medical examiner finally released her to us," Trace says. "We're taking her back to Atlanta tomorrow for her . . . funeral. God, man, I can't . . . We'll come back when you need us to, but anything we can do today."

He keeps speaking for everyone who was in the house that night, but I wonder if he really can.

"Where is Ashley?" I ask.

"Her mother's place," he says. "Brett's there too. We all were for a while, but . . . I couldn't take it anymore. She's got a small place and her son still lives there with his kid and . . ."

"Why didn't Ashley come here with you?"

"She's going to tonight, I think. Didn't want to hurt her mom's feelings by all leaving at once or something. I'm not sure."

"Where is Nadine?"

"She went back to Atlanta yesterday," he says. "Start getting things ready for our return and the . . . funeral and stuff."

"We asked y'all to stay here so we could—"

"She'd already been interviewed," he says. "We're all leaving tomorrow. She'll come back anytime you need her to. She's the nanny."

"We wanted to talk to everyone again before y'all left," I say, "including her."

"I can get her back by tonight," he says. "I'll fly her down, but I'm tellin' you no one staying with us had anything to do with . . . what happened to Mariah."

"Know how you asked me not to focus on y'all so much that I didn't look at anyone else?" I say.

"Yeah?"

"You need to do the opposite. Don't be so certain it was an intruder that you're completely closed to it being someone staying in the house that night. There are no signs of forced entry and when a child is killed the chance of it being a family member or someone close to the family are extremely high."

"Fair point," he says. "But . . . there's no way anyone of us did that to Mariah. No way."

"And if we find out it was one of them?"

"I'll hack them into tiny pieces with the dullest knife I can find and burn the bits to ash myself. Don't care which one of 'em it is."

21

"It wasn't any of us," Hunter says. "No doubt in my mind. So there won't be any need for hacking anybody. None of us could do what was done to little Mariah. You know that, man. Come on."

"Did either of you hear anything that night?" I ask.

"Wish to God I had," Trace says. "Give anything to have heard something. But I was wiped. Stayed up all night the night before, then spent all day with the family and fireworks. Turned in early and when I did, people were still shootin' off fireworks down on the beach, but soon as my head hit the pillow, I never heard another sound."

I look over at Hunter.

He shakes his head. "Nothin' out of the ordinary."

"Either of you hear the elevator come up late in the night?" I ask.

Hunter nods. "But that's not out of the ordinary."

"Who would be on it that late?" Trace asks. "None of us really used it. The kids played in it a little when we first got there, but after that . . ."

Hunter shrugs. "Don't know. I just think I remember hearing it while I was sending the last of my emails before lights out."

Trace looks at me. "Did the killer use the elevator? That why you're askin'?"

"Just askin'," I say. "Have no reason to think so."

I glance back at Merrill. He's yet to utter a single sound.

He gives me the slightest of nods.

"How about Mariah's mother?" I ask. "Never hear anything about her. Do you have sole custody?"

Hunter shakes his head and lets out an expression of disgust. "Mayra," he says.

"She died when Mariah was very small," Trace says. "OD'd. Her family blamed me, accused me of killing her, said if I didn't actually murder her, which they think I did, that at a minimum I got her hooked on the shit in the first place. Her parents, Pick and Rhonda Baxley and her sister, Deidre, fought me for custody. I've had nothing to do with them since."

"They who you need to look at," Irvin says, his voice rising.

Trace shakes his head. "They could no more hurt Mariah than I could. They're broken—all of them. Older than their years. Losing a daughter—" He stops suddenly and tears fill his eyes again. "Sure that's the way I'll be soon. Oh, God. I just can't . . . believe she's . . . They wouldn't harm her. They're decent people —all three of them. They could've tried to take her or harm her when I was in prison if they were going to, but they didn't. Now, I'm sure you'll talk to them. Just remember they blame me for their daughter's death. No telling what all they'll tell you about me. Just remember it's their grief talkin'. I was young and stupid and selfish when I was with their daughter and I made a lot of mistakes, but I didn't kill her. Just like I didn't kill their grand-daughter."

"Know who you really need to be lookin' at," Hunter says.

"Who?" I say.

He looks at Trace. "Who has the biggest beef with you on the planet?"

Trace shakes his head. "He wouldn't do something like this, not to Mariah, just to get at me."

"Who?" I say.

"Little Swag," Hunter says. "Biggest beef in rap right now. He's threatened to do something like this and more."

"In his songs," Trace says. "It's not an actual threat."

"The hell it's not," Hunter says. "Fucker ain't like you. He's crazy. He's street hard and crack crazy. Means what he says in his songs and you know it. And he's killed before."

I look at Trace.

"I'm not sayin' you shouldn't look at him. I want you lookin' at everybody. I just . . . It's hard to imagine anyone doing this, so . . . I can't picture him or anyone else doing what was done to my baby."

"Give me a little backstory," I say.

"He's another Atlanta rapper. We used to collaborate," Trace says. "He was part of our posse. When things took off for me, he wanted to take the ride with me. I tried to give him a few things here and there, but he thought they were beneath him. He wanted to be on my new record. Wanted me on his. Wanted me to get him a spot on a TV show I was on."

"His punk ass took it public," Hunter says. "Spittin' all kind of dark, twisted rhymes about my boy here. And he never been anything but good to him. Made all kinds of threats. Tried to take him out a couple of months ago."

I look back at Trace.

"Drive-by at a club in Buckhead," he says. "We were standing out front, but so were a lot of other people. Don't know it was for us. And . . ."

"And what?"

He shrugs. "I don't know. Seemed like the guy wasn't really

trying to hit anybody. Could've easily taken us out. Nobody got hit. Sort of shot up over the top of us."

"You think it was him?"

"If it was, it sort of proves my point about him really not wanting to hurt anyone," he says. "I just don't think he would."

Hunter shakes his head and lets out a harsh laugh. "And you never been wrong about something like that before?"

Trace nods slowly. "Fair point there. Not saying I'm always the best judge of character. Keep you around, don't I?"

"I'm bein' serious," Hunter says. "Tryin' to protect you and find out who did what was done . . ."

"You're right. Like I said, look into him. I'm all for it. Just hate to see another brother get accused of something he's innocent of."

"John won't do that," Merrill says.

They are his first and last words of the entire conversation.

"I'm assuming Little Swag isn't the name his mama gave him," I say. "What's his legal handle?"

"Rondarius," Trace says. "Rondarius Swaggart."

22

F ilicide is the act of killing one's own child.

And though it shouldn't be a thing we need a name for, it's far more common than we'd like to think.

In the U.S. alone each year, between 450 and 500 children are intentionally murdered by a parent. Of those, over seventy percent are kids six years old and under. In well over half of all cases, the father is the killer.

Though he seems to be cooperating, and said all the right things, I leave Trace Evers' rented home on the river wondering if he's one of those fathers.

And as I drive toward the home Ashley Howard grew up in, I wonder if Trace didn't do it, if she did.

Somewhere in America a mother murders her child every three days.

Though not Mariah's mother or even stepmother, Ashley certainly seems to be filling that role.

I don't know a lot about Ashley Howard yet, but what I know, I find interesting and instructive.

She grew up poor in Wewa.

Her parents, who were both alcoholics, bought a lakeside

lodge with cabins for rent and a boat launch called Dead Lakes Roadside Inn and through mismanagement and neglect let the property go to wreck and ruin, and the business died a slow, ugly death.

Growing up, Ashley, as if familiar with the AA slogan *Fake it 'til you make it,* always acted like the rich, popular girl she wanted to be.

And she was pretty and poised enough to get away with it.

She shoplifted the clothes and shoes and jewelry she couldn't afford and became an adroit social climber.

At twenty-seven she still has what I've heard described as a bikini body—nice, natural curves, tone, tight, and muscular, with only the slightest hint of a mom tummy, something I think makes her more not less attractive.

It's July and it's hot, but she's not dressed like it. Unlike in nearly every other picture I've seen her in, she's wearing long pants and long sleeves—old blue jeans and a Wewa Gators sweatshirt.

In addition to showing off her body, Ashley normally wears clothes cut to show off the various ink she has on that body.

Everything else is the same—the perfect blond hair, the carefully applied makeup, the exquisite jewelry—which makes the clothes standout all the more.

We're sitting on the back porch of one of the dilapidated old cabins with a truly magnificent view of the Dead Lakes.

It's not raining yet, but dark thunderheads can be seen in the distance.

"I'm still in shock," she says. "You know what I mean? Not as in surprised or like shocked that it happened, but like in shock because it did happen."

"You're not surprised that it happened?" I ask.

"Not particularly, no," she says. "I told Trace putting her in that video and have her come up on stage all the time and posting so many pictures with her was a bad idea. It's like an invitation to deranged and damaged people. You can't advertise something and think people won't want it."

A slight breeze ripples the surface of the water and sways the Spanish moss in the cypress trees.

"Even if some sick kiddie diddler hadn't come for her," she says, "it was just bad for a child that small to get that kind of attention and . . . all. But he was always trying to make up for her mama dying and him being sent away."

I nod.

Before us the flooded cypress trees of the Dead Lakes stand jagged and craggy, their bases hidden beneath the tannic waters.

"It's funny, he's got this tough guy image, but he's not very street smart at all. Not at all. I'm more . . . than he is. If it were up to me I wouldn't be talkin' to you right now, but he's convinced if we cooperate you'll clear us and get on with finding out who really did it. He's too trusting. He wouldn't even have a lawyer if it wasn't for me."

"So why are you talkin' to me?" I ask.

"'Cause Trace wants me to," she says. "I have nothin' to hide, but I know enough to know that doesn't mean shit if y'all decide we did it and decide to build a case against us."

"I'm truly trying to find out what happened," I say, "to gather information and follow the facts of the case no matter where they lead. This isn't about clearing or closing a case for me. Never is. If you don't want to talk to me, you don't have to, but if you're willing . . . tell me about the night of the Fourth."

She does, and it's almost identical to what Trace and Irvin Hunter said.

"You didn't get up during the night?" I ask.

She shakes her head.

"Didn't hear anything?"

"Didn't wake up until Nadine banged on our door with Mariah's note saying she had run away."

"How about the elevator?" I ask. "Did you hear it that night?"

"Just told you I didn't even stir."

"Tell me about Mariah," I say.

I'm interested in her feelings about and relationship with Mariah.

I have the Cinderella effect in mind—the evolutionary psychology theory for why there is a higher rate of mistreatment and abuse by stepparents than biological ones.

Interestingly, though mistreatment and abuse by stepparents seems to be higher, murder by them is much, much lower. Only ten percent of the children killed by parents in the US each year are killed by stepparents.

And yet two lines from Mariah's runaway note keep echoing through my mind. *Ashley and Brett or to mean to me. I love them but cannot take it.*

"She was a good girl—especially given everything she had been through," she says. "Lost her mom forever. Lost her dad for a few years. Don't get me wrong, she had issues, but . . . given her . . . situation."

"What kinds of issues?" I ask.

"The usual kid stuff—attitude, stubbornness, lying, disobedience, that sort of thing. And she was spoiled. Trace always felt so much guilt about . . . well, everything, that he spoiled the shit out of that child. It's a miracle she wasn't worse than what she was. To her credit, she didn't take advantage of it too much. That says a lot for a child that young. 'Course she got nearly all of her daddy's attention and everything she wanted, so . . ."

She sounds jealous, and I wonder if it's a factor in what happened.

"Did she have a phone?" I ask. "We didn't find one among her things."

She shakes her head. "Only two things he didn't let her get . . . a phone and her ears pierced. She wanted both bad, but he told her she had to wait and he stuck with it. Don't know why exactly. But he did. His way of keeping control or tellin' himself he was you know like parenting. Bet he regrets it now. And the thing is . . . he let her have an iPod. She couldn't make calls, but hell, who calls anymore? She could text anybody with an iPhone. And actually, Brett said she had an app that let her text anybody period."

I didn't remember seeing an iPod on the evidence inventory, but I need to double check. Reading her texts could be extremely helpful or a complete waste of time—either way we'd need to do it if we can locate her device.

"What was your relationship with her like? I ask.

"Trace and I decided a long time ago that I would parent my kid and he'd parent his," she says. "We aren't married or anything yet, so it's not like we're their stepparents or anything yet, so . . . it just worked better. We're different and we're different with our kids."

"So y'all weren't close?"

She shrugs. "We were close enough. She was closer to Nadine. She was the closest thing to a mother the poor child ever had. Don't get me wrong, we got along fine. I just didn't try to pretend to be her mother."

"Who handled the discipline?"

"What discipline?" she says. "There was none. Trace didn't do it and certainly wouldn't let anyone else do it. Not even Nadine—though I think she and the little princess had an understanding."

I nod.

She looks at me, her eyes locking onto mine. "I know what her little runaway note said, but . . . I wasn't mean to her. Neither was Brett. I was great to her. Treated her better than her own mother ever did, and besides the normal sibling scuffles . . . she and Brett got along just fine."

"And she got no discipline?" I ask.

"But there again . . ." she says. "It shows what a good kid she was that with very little discipline and having her daddy wrapped around her little finger that she was as good as she was."

"Can you think of anyone who might have killed her?" I ask.

She shakes her head. "Absolutely not. She was a small child for God's sakes. Who kills a child? I mean, really. Who? The mentally deranged, right? I have no idea who it could be. I don't think I know anyone capable of something like that."

When the rain comes, the wind comes with it, blowing the cold raindrops in at an angle on us under the porch.

Since I need to talk to Brett next anyway, we make a dash for her mom's sad little house.

And that's when I see it.

As she's running and as we dry off inside her mom's mudroom, the ends of her sleeves and pant cuffs shift enough for me to see what's beneath them.

They are light and they are subtle, but they are there.

In addition to all her other tattoos, Ashley Howard has images of ropes around her wrists and ankles not unlike the ones around the dead body of Mariah when she was found.

23

"You'd think with all the money they have, she'd buy her mom a decent place to live, wouldn't you?"

The question comes from Arlene LaFontaine, Ashley's mom, as we are drying off.

She yells it from the recliner in the living room, surrounded by stacks of newspapers and cats.

"I keep telling her it's Trace's money, not mine," Ashley says to me, "but it doesn't matter."

From the small, dim kitchen that smells of poorly ventilated propane, Ashley's brother says, "I told you we don't need any of that . . . man's money, Ma. Not that he'd share it with us anyway. Hell, I don't think he gives much to Ashley. Besides, I've got some things that are about to come through. We're gonna be fine."

Ashley rolls her eyes. "He's had some things about to come through for a decade now. He's just like them."

The small, dingy house is cluttered and unclean, and has the sour smell of stale sweat, cigarette smoke, and cat urine.

"Brett," Ashley calls, raising her voice. "Honey, come here."

To me she says, "We can talk in the dining room."

She leads me into the living room where her overweight and

whiskey-old mom in ill-fitting Dollar Store clothes is watching a rerun of *Murder, She Wrote* a little too loudly.

"I always say . . . I like this town just fine," Arlene says, "but if Jessica Fletcher ever moves here, I'm gone. Everywhere she goes there's a murder."

"It's because she's a serial killer," I say. "That's her thing. She frames other people for her kills."

"Huh?" she says, squinting up at me beneath a tangle of too early graying hair.

"Nothin', Ma," Hank says from the kitchen. "He was pulling your leg."

Hank Howard, Jr. comes to the doorway of the kitchen in sweatpants and a wife beater, a frying pan in one hand, a spatula in the other. A few years Ashley's junior, he looks to be about twenty years older.

"You guys want some eggs?" he says. "I'm making some eggs."

"I'm good, thanks," I say.

Ashley shakes her head. "No, thanks."

"Don't know what you're missin'. I put some cheese and cayenne in them. Ask little Brett if he wants some."

"He's allergic to dairy and doesn't like spicy food," Ashley says.

"Oh. Okay. More for me and Ma."

"Where is he?" Ashley says. "Brett. Come in here, honey."

A skinny, young, blond boy appears at the opening to the hallway.

"Where were you, baby?"

"In my room."

"Oh, it's your room now, is it?" Hank yells from the kitchen.

"Come in the dining room, honey," Ashley says. "This policeman has some questions to ask you about Mariah."

She leads the two of us into the small dining room and the three of us sit at the far end of the table—as far away from the living room and Arlene, Hank, and Jessica Fletcher as we can get —which is not nearly far enough.

"I'm very sorry about what happened to Mariah," I say. "I'm trying to find out exactly what that was and why. Do you mind answering some questions for me?"

He shrugs.

"It's okay, baby," Ashley says. "Just like we talked about. Answer the questions for Mommy, okay?"

"Did you like Mariah?" I ask.

He shrugs.

"Was she fun to play with?"

He shrugs again but then nods too.

"She . . . didn't like . . . video games," he says.

"Brett loves video games," Ashley says. "They're his favorite thing to do."

"You do?" I say.

He nods. "Yes, sir."

"What's your favorite?"

"Right now . . . ah . . . Minecraft."

"Cool."

"You ever played it?" he asks.

I shake my head. "Not yet, but I hear everybody talking about it. Should I try it?"

He nods. "Uh huh. It's the best."

"You build things with it, right?" Ashley says.

He nods.

"Can we talk about Mariah?" I say. "Are you sad about what happened to her?"

He hesitates, looks at his mom, then nods.

"Do you know what happened to her or who might have done it?"

He shakes his head, glances at his mom, then shakes it more vigorously.

"Did you enjoy the party the night before the Fourth?" I ask.

He shrugs.

"What did y'all do when you went upstairs?"

"Played."

"Who played what?"

He shrugs and twists his lips and raises his eyebrows. "Not sure . . . what all. I played Minecraft."

"I'm tellin' you he's obsessed with that game," Ashley says.

"Anybody play it with you?"

"Caden for a little while then he left."

"Where'd he go?"

Again the shrug. "Play with Mariah I think. She and Miss Nadine were playin' Connect Four or somethin'. Said he didn't just want to sit and watch me play Minecraft."

"You didn't let him have a turn?" Ashley asks.

"Wasn't his turn yet."

"We always let the guest go first, okay?" she says. "From now on."

He nods. "Yes, ma'am."

"Did you enjoy the fireworks in town the next night?"

He shrugs again, and I wonder why he doesn't have more developed shoulder and neck muscles.

"Did you hear anything after y'all came in from launching fireworks on the beach?" I ask.

He shrugs.

"You either do or you don't, baby," Ashley says. "Tell the detective everything you can remember."

"Miss Nadine said you were still up when she went to bed," I say.

"She's not supposed to do that," Ashley says. "Go to bed while they're still awake."

"She said you were playing video games in your room," I say. "How late did you stay up?"

He shrugs again. "Not sure. Not too late. I was tired, but wanted to play some Minecraft before I went to sleep."

"Did anything happen?" I ask. "Did you leave your room for any reason?"

He shakes his head.

"Did you see anyone? Hear anything?"

He shakes his head. "Not while I was playing, but . . . after I laid down."

"What'd you hear?"

"I thought I heard—something woke me up. I thought it was Mariah. Sometimes we'd get up and sneak downstairs for snacks or to go play on the beach."

"While we were asleep?" Ashley says. "Did the nanny go with you?"

He nods at her first questions and shakes his head at the second.

"Was it Mariah?" I ask.

He shakes his head. "No one was there. I then heard a noise like maybe she was on the stairs. Figured she tried to wake me then went down without me. I don't know."

"Was anyone else ever around when y'all went out and played at night?" I ask.

He shakes his head. "Sometimes Caden or Beau would meet us."

"Caden Stevens the boy staying next door?" I ask.

He nods. "He and Mariah liked each other."

"They did?"

"More than they liked me."

"They just liked playing different games," Ashley says. "It's not you. They like you."

"Who is Beau?"

"His family was staying on the other side of our place, but they left before the Fourth," Ashley says. "I'm not even sure of his last name."

"Did you get up to go see if it was Mariah on the stairs?" I ask.

He shakes his head.

"Did you hear the elevator being used that night?"

He shakes his head.

"Did you hear or see anything else that night?" I ask. "Anything at all?"

He shrugs. "No, sir."

"Nothing?" Ashley asks. "You sure?"

He nods. "I thought I saw a man pass by out in the hallway," he says, "but it was just a dream. Nobody was there."

"When?" she asks before I can. "What'd he look like? Why didn't you tell Mommy?"

"It was just a bad dream."

"Why do you think it was a dream?" I ask.

He shrugs.

"It's important," I say. "Please try to remember. Why did you think it was just dream?"

"His . . . face. He . . . he didn't have a face."

"What do you mean, sweetie?" Ashley says.

He shrugs. "I don't know. I . . . Sometimes in bad dreams people don't have faces."

"Sometimes in real life too," I say.

24

"What do you think he meant?" Anna asks. "A man with no face."

"I don't know," I say. "He really could have just been dreaming. Could've been part of a nightmare."

"But if he wasn't," she says. "If he really saw someone."

"A mask maybe," I say.

On my way back to a meeting with Reggie, Arnie, and Keisha, I've made a quick detour by our home to kiss my wife.

We're standing in the shade of the oak trees near the end of our driveway—oak trees still wet from the afternoon shower, their bark dark with water, raindrops glistening on their leaves, dripping intermittently onto the damp soil below.

Inside our home, while Taylor naps, Johanna is helping Sam and Daniel pack. When Anna and I finish making out and talking, we'll go in to see them and wake Taylor up.

We're all going to miss Sam and Daniel living with us—probably far more than any of us even realize.

"If the hallway was dark and the killer had on a black ski mask . . ." she says.

"Absolutely," I say. "That could absolutely be it. Or one of those Halloween masks that are blank—featureless, colorless, expressionless."

"Does a mask mean someone broke in?" she says.

"It could," I say. "Can't be sure he even saw it, but if he really did . . . I'd say that might mean it was more likely an intruder. Of course, there's no evidence of a break in and until all the evidence is processed, we won't know if there's anything at all to indicate even the possibility someone else was in the house."

"Of course the presence of a mask doesn't necessarily mean it wasn't someone from inside the house," she says.

"True."

"Someone sick enough to tie up and murder a child like that . . ."

"Mask could be part of his fantasy," I say. "Or ritual. And if he didn't plan on killing her, it could've been to conceal his identity."

"Someone from inside the house or an intruder," she says, "who does something like this?"

It's rhetorical, which is good, because it's not a question I can answer.

Though it is generally accepted that there are three theories and five reasons for why parents kill their children, they don't begin to touch on the inexplicable evil that is filicide.

The three theories are mental illness, abnormally high levels of testosterone, and unwanted offspring.

There are five major reasons for filicide.

Altruism—the parent kills the child because of the belief that it is in their best interest.

Acute psychosis—the parent murders the child based on a belief not consistent with reality, such as the child is evil or dangerous.

An unwanted child—the parent kills the child because he or she is considered to be an undue burden or hindrance.

Accident—the child's death is unintentional or an unintended consequence of parental physical abuse.

Spousal revenge—the parent kills the child as an act of aggression or spite against the other parent.

As sound and sort of obvious as these theories and reasons are, they are powerless to explain what is beyond comprehension.

"With or without the mask," she says, "he's a monster."

25

"So the ropes used to tie up Mariah . . ." Jessica says.

"Before we get to that," I say. "I don't see an iPod listed among Mariah's things or in the evidence inventory log."

Jessica shakes her head. "There wasn't one."

"Ashley says she had one that she used like a phone—could text with it, which she was evidently doing all the time."

"It wasn't in the house," Jessica says. "Not anywhere."

"Then we've got to assume her killer took it," Reggie says. "Must have something incriminating on it."

We all grow quiet as we think about it and make a note of it for our case files.

"So . . . the ropes . . ." Jessica says.

"Yes," Reggie says.

"They're Shibari or Japanese bondage ropes. Black. Soft cotton. Imported from Japan. Ten meters long. Eight millimeters in diameter."

Of all sexual bondage, Japanese bondage is considered by many to be the most artistic and beautiful.

"The package the ropes come in says that it's multifunctional," Jessica says, then looks down at her notes. "'This rope can be used for tying luggage, bedroom fantasies, games, sewing, craft projects, costume playing and organizing. It's also great as a soft bondage rope for adult restraint fun.'"

"Funny how they put that as almost an afterthought," Keisha says.

"Yeah," Jessica says, "these are made for one thing and one thing only—and it ain't tying up luggage."

Arnie, Keisha, Jessica, and I are with Reggie in her office, discussing the case, sharing what we've found with the others.

Arnie, whose face is flushed, appears particularly uncomfortable.

Jessica passes around crime scene photos of Mariah once the blanket she had been wrapped in had been removed.

Thankfully, and surprisingly, Mariah is in her bathing suit.

"Five ropes were used on Mariah," Jessica says. "Three full lengths and two half lengths. Her ankles were bound together and her wrists bound together behind her back, then the two were tied to each other. Then what is known as a harness was tied around her chest, upper arms, and neck."

The photographs show a young girl who appears to be sleeping, bound by elaborately wrapped and knotted ropes. Both the types of ropes and the way they're tied are obviously sexual, and would look artistic and erotic on an adult female form, but on a child they look simultaneously absurd and abhorrent.

"What kind of sick, sadistic fuck would do shit like this to a child?" Keisha says.

"That *is* the question," Reggie says.

I notice Arnie passes the pictures without looking at them, and keeps his gaze averted from wherever the photos might be.

"You okay?" Reggie asks.

"I can't look at this," Arnie says.

"We have to," Reggie says.

"I can't. You can reassign me if you want to, but I just can't. I saw some of it at the scene, but I can't look at it any more. I have a granddaughter about her age and . . ."

"It's okay," she says.

"You're having a normal reaction," I say. "None of us want to look at them. It's okay."

"You don't have to look at them," Reggie says. "It's fine."

"I won't look away," Keisha says. "I want them seared into my brain so that the only thing that can replace it is the guy who did it shot in the face."

"This looks pretty elaborate," I say. "Not just the position of the ropes, but the way the knots are tied. I'm assuming this would take some time and have to be done by someone who has done this before."

Jessica nods. "Looks more complicated than it is, but obviously someone would have to know what they're doing. Probably done it before. Or read about it. Tons of videos online tell you just how to do it. There are three common knots from bondage that are used—the overhand, the reef or square not, and the Lark's Head."

"They're common to other things too," Arnie says.

Jessica nods.

"Are we thinking this is some sick sexual crime and that the murder may or may not have been part of the original plan?" Keisha says.

"It's obviously sexual," Reggie says. "And according to the ME she was molested."

"But not around the time of her death," I say.

"Based on what the ME said," Keisha adds, "maybe he was intending to molest or rape her but something made him kill her before he could."

"She could've been unconscious and woke up and began to scream or fight him," Reggie says.

"The question is," Keisha says, "does that argue more for an intruder or someone already in the house?"

"Like John pointed out," Reggie says, "this would take a while —which would seem to point toward someone in the house. But it has to be someone who knows how to do it."

"Hopefully when we get the DNA results back on the ropes, it'll tell us who it was," Jessica says, "but—"

"When I was interviewing Ashley Howard today," I say, "I noticed she has tattoos of ropes that look a lot like these on her wrists and ankles."

"I can do you one better than that," Keisha says. "Look at this."

She taps her tablet and a video begins playing. As she holds it up, we all lean in so we can see it.

A sexy, sultry music video fills the screen.

Two figures on an enormous silk-sheet-covered bed in a candlelit room.

In it, as he sings and raps graphically about all the ways he wants to have sex with her, Trace is tying a partially clothed Ashley up with ropes like the ones used on Mariah.

"Oh my God," Arnie says.

"Are we watching a confession?" Reggie says.

"Y'all've never seen this?" Keisha says. "It's pretty popular."

"That's a wrap, folks," Arnie says. "Case closed."

"Told you I could do you one better," Keisha says. "Aren't ya'll glad you got a sister on the case? How long would it have taken you white folk to find that?"

"I can do you both one better," Jessica says.

"The ropes actually used on Mariah belong to Trace and Ashley," she says.

She pauses for a long moment to let that sink in.

"We found ropes in what can only be described as their sex kit," she says. "A little overnight bag with toys and lube and masks and cuffs and stuff—and in her suitcase."

"That does look very suspicious," Arnie says, "but that doesn't mean the ropes used on Mariah belonged to them."

"I'm sure the DNA tests will confirm it," she says, "but we don't need them to. Remember how I said five ropes were used? Three full lengths and two half lengths. Well the half lengths were just a full length cut in half. Thing is . . . they weren't two halves of the same full length piece. They were each one half of two different full length pieces. And . . . the two other matching halves . . . they were found in Ashley's suitcase."

26

"I miss Sam and Daniel being here," Anna says.

"I do too."

It's late. The girls have long since said prayers and been tucked in, and Anna and I are in bed in our dark room, whispering our final few words of the day.

I don't mention it to Anna, but in addition to missing Sam and Daniel's presence in our home, I will miss having another armed adult to help respond to Chris when he makes his move.

"I know they have a ways to go," she says, "but I'm amazed at how well they're doing. So happy they're together again and have hope for a future."

"A short while ago it didn't seem possible," I say.

"Her returning him unharmed makes me think Randa's not all bad," she says.

"She's not. Part of what makes her so interesting is what a contradiction she is."

"So you don't think she's a sociopath?"

I shake my head, though in the dimness, I'm not sure she can see it. "No, I don't. I've certainly wondered from time to time, but . . . I don't believe she is."

Anna yawns, bringing the back of her hand up to cover her mouth. "Better kiss me goodnight before I—" she begins, then yawns again.

"Sounds like I better time it just right," I say.

"It's safe now," she says. "Go for it."

She lifts her head and turns toward me. I meet her and we kiss. And though I'm sure it's not possible, it seems as though she's asleep by the time she lays her head back down.

Sleep didn't come as quickly for me, but when it did arrive, dreams arrived with it.

It's the early morning hours of December 26, 1996.

A frantic 911 call from 755 15th Street in Boulder, Colorado, but instead of Patsy Ramsey, it's Ashley Howard placing the call.

755 Fifteenth Street.

What is going on there ma'am?

We have a kidnapping...Hurry, please.

Explain to me what is going on, okay?

We have a . . . There's a note left and our daughter is gone.

A note was left and your daughter is gone?

Yes.

How old is your daughter?

She is six years old. She is blond. Six years old.

How long ago was this?

I don't know. Just found a note and my daughter is missing.

Does it say who took her?

What?

Does it say who took her?

No I don't know. It's there . . . there is a ransom note here.

It's a ransom note.

It says S.B.T.C. Victory. Please.

Okay. What's your name? Are you...

Ashley Howard. I'm the mother. Oh my God. Please.

Okay. I'm sending an officer over, okay?

Please.

Do you know how long she's been gone?

No, I don't. Please. We just got up and she's not here. Oh my God Please.

Okay.

Please send somebody.

I am, honey.

Please.

Take a deep breath.

Hurry. Hurry. Hurry.

Ashley? Ashley? Ashley? Ashley? Ashley?

Suddenly I'm on the stairs leading to the basement, passing the broken window, the scuff mark on the wall, the blue suitcase below.

And then the door.

And beyond the door on the floor, the lifeless body of a child beauty queen.

Door flung open.

White blanket on the floor, blond hair visible at the top.

Rushing over, hoping it's not too late, knowing that it is.

Removing duct tape from her mouth, her skin cold to the touch.

I wake up thinking about how different Mariah's restraints were from JonBenét's.

Small white cords versus thick black ropes.

And the way they were used.

In addition to having her hands and feet tied with the narrow white cord, JonBenét was garroted with it, her small body showing signs of violence—especially her head and neck. A deep ligature furrow and petechial hemorrhages around her neck. Abrasions and petechial hemorrhages on the face.

Mariah was bound with soft Japanese bondage ropes in a way that can only be described as sexual, but there were no signs of violence.

Both children are dead, but one's death seems to have been far more violent and brutal.

"Do you want to just move their beds into our room for a while?" Anna whispers.

She has once again found me asleep on the floor of the girls' room, center of the floor, equal distance between Taylor's baby bed and Johanna's big girl bed.

I smile up at her. "It's not just the case," I say. "It's Chris and not knowing what he might do."

She nods. "I know."

Like the last time, she disappears for a moment and returns with pillows, a blanket, and my phone.

Lying down beside me, she says, "We'll sleep in here tonight and tomorrow we'll move their beds into our room."

"If it would make you feel better," I say.

She laughs out loud at that, but fortunately not loud enough to wake the girls.

27

I wake the next morning stiff from sleeping on the floor, wanting to compare other aspects of Mariah and JonBenét's cases.

At the kitchen table, over a bowl of Frosted Flakes, I read and reread the three notes and think about and compare them with each other, glancing occasionally to the spot in the living room where Sam's hospital bed used to be.

D ear Dad,
    Ashley and Brett or to mean to me. I love them but cannot take it. I sorry for leaving you like this. Y'all all will be happy with out me. Please do not look for me. I will be fine. I will miss.
    Love you, Mariah.

A re we dealing with a runaway, a kidnaping, a murder, or some combination? Did Mariah really run away or try to? Was she killed while attempting to? Or could the note have been from an earlier or for a later time? If she was running away, why?

Was it just for the reasons listed in her note or was there more to it? Was someone helping her or going with her or was it just her? And where was she running to?

I'll make this simple so even an ignorant thug like you can understand. I have your daughter. If you want her back it will cost you $250,000.00. That's a very small amount because I want to do this fast and easy. I know you have a lot more, but that's all I want. I'm not greedy, have no desire to be nigger rich like you. I don't want no gold teeth or spinning rims or any shit like that. Your song says you will never leave her again. Well, maybe not, but she's left you. You say you will never hurt her again, never let her down. We will see if you really mean that. I don't want to hurt your little girl. Don't make me. Just gather the money and I'll call you with where we'll meet to make the trade. Don't test me boy. Don't call the police. Don't tell anyone. You do and it's lights out for the little mixed girl. Just get the little chump change together and wait for my call. Be smarter than you seem and don't fuck this up. Your little girl's life depends on it.

Unlike the Ramsey ransom letter, the note left on Mariah's bed isn't addressed to anyone—though it's obviously directed toward Trace. The relatively brief note isn't just threatening, it's demeaning and insulting too. Its lack of salutation to Trace seems another obvious dis, another form of contempt. Like the Ramsey note, the demand is for a relatively small amount of money, but unlike the Ramsey note, the Evers note explains why.

And now to what has been called the *War and Peace* of ransom notes:

Mr. Ramsey,
Listen carefully! We are a group of individuals that represent a small foreign faction. We do respect your bussiness but not the country that it serves. At this time we have your daughter in our posession. She is safe and unharmed and if you want her to see 1997, you must follow our instructions to the letter.

You will withdraw $118,000.00 from your account. $100,000 will be in $100 bills and the remaining $18,000 in $20 bills. Make sure that you bring an adequate size attache to the bank. When you get home you will put the money in a brown paper bag. I will call you between 8 and 10 am tomorrow to instruct you on delivery. The delivery will be exhausting so I advise you to be rested. If we monitor you getting the money early, we might call you early to arrange an earlier delivery of the money and hence a earlier delivery pick-up of your daughter.

Any deviation of my instructions will result in the immediate execution of your daughter. You will also be denied her remains for proper burial. The two gentlemen watching over your daughter do not particularly like you so I advise you not to provoke them. Speaking to anyone about your situation, such as Police, F.B.I., etc., will result in your daughter being beheaded. If we catch you talking to a stray dog, she dies. If you alert bank authorities, she dies. If the money is in any way marked or tampered with, she dies. You will be scanned for electronic devices and if any are found, she dies. You can try to deceive us but be warned that we are familiar with law enforcement countermeasures and tactics. You stand a 99% chance of killing your daughter if you try to out smart us. Follow our instructions and you stand a 100% chance of getting her back.

You and your family are under constant scrutiny as well as the authorities. Don't try to grow a brain John. You are not the only fat cat around so don't think that killing will be difficult. Don't underestimate us John. Use that good southern common sense of yours. It is up to you now John!

Victory!

S.B.T.C

Though there are many, many notable differences in the two cases, one of the main features they have in common, apart from little girls who performed in public, is the presence of a ransom note at a scene where the child was not actually taken from the house. Who leaves a ransom note and a body? Who murders the person they are attempting to leverage for ransom?

Another interesting component that is similar in a way but different is the use of movie lines in the Ramsey note and song lines or at least references in the Evers note.

In addition to the amount of money demanded in each note being relatively low—most kidnapers demand millions—the amount in the Ramsey letter is both specific and bizarre. Only $118,000.00 demanded of a millionaire whose company is worth billions. Two main theories have been posited—that the amount was almost exactly the amount of John Ramsey's annual bonus that year or that the amount would convert into one million pesos in Mexico at the time—but neither is completely convincing or begins to explain either the oddity of the sum or the motivation behind it.

Why is the Ramsey note so long?

Why were both the Ramsey and the Evers notes left along with the bodies?

Why was the Evers note left along with Mariah's runaway note?

Most experts agree that it would be nearly impossible for the murderer to write the notes after the murders—especially one as long as the Ramsey note, which had to be written in the Ramsey house around the time of the murder, because it was written with a pen on a pad that belonged to the Ramseys found in their home.

28

"Did time with your boy in Georgia," Chance Hill says.

We are in my office in the chapel of Gulf Correctional Institution where I work part-time.

Chance Hill, an inmate who evidently is doing an incarceration tour of the Southern states, is a short, thin, African-American in his mid-thirties who looks far more like a boy than a man.

"My boy?" I say.

"Evidence," he says. "Trace. Trace *Evidence* Evers." He shakes his head. "*Evidence*. Ain't that some shit? Gave himself that name when we's stackin' time near Atlanta. Said he leaves evidence of Trace on all the shorties."

From the back of the building, the sounds of Muslim prayers drift through the chapel like peaceful Persian poetry being sung leisurely in the languid meridian of a hot, dusty day, and I can picture the Imam and the Islamic inmates in socked-feet and kufis on their prayer rugs in the fellowship hall.

Allāhu ʾakbar
ʾašhadu ʾan lā ʾilāha ʾillā Llāh
ʾašhadu ʾanna Muḥammadan rasūlu Llāh

"Why do you say he's my boy?" I ask.

"Word on the 'pound is you investigatin' him in your other job."

Though I shouldn't be, I'm continually amazed at the information inmates have access to and how it spreads into every corner and crevice of the compound.

"Media goin' crazy over this case," he says. "Reportin' all kinda shit. No way it can all be true, but even if half of it is . . ."

Allāhu ʾakbar

Chance is often bringing me information, mostly rumors and gossip. Until now they've been mostly about the prison—the goings on of inmates, correctional officers, and staff. He's like the prison town crier, making pronouncements, passing along information useful and not. Mostly not. But I've never dissuaded him because on occasion his information has been extremely helpful.

"Soon as I heard I knew I had to tell you what I knew about him," he says. "You do time with a man . . . you learn a lot about 'im. A lot. And Trace is dangerous. Just not in the way you might think."

Allāhu ʾakbar

"What do you mean?" I ask.

"He's not dangerous in like a thug way, like the way he fronts in his songs and videos and shit. He's more dangerous in a sneaky, kinda psychological way."

ʾašhadu ʾan lā ʾilāha ʾillā Llāh
ʾašhadu ʾanna Muḥammadan rasūlu Llāh

"Can you unpack that a little for me?" I ask.

"You talk to him yet?" he says. "Bet if you have, he told you everything you wanted to hear, didn't he? He's like that. Scary good at reading a room and becoming just what he needs to be. You'll see. He can be a thug, a caring, sensitive guy, daddy of the year, contrite, defiant, all about love and unity or a radical racist ready to burn White America to the ground."

I don't say anything. Through my office window I can see the late-afternoon sun low in the sky, sinking toward evening, and the goldish-orange glow it casts on the buildings and the inmates and staff walking between them.

"I like you, Chaplain," he says. "You'a positive in this equation up in here. Just wanted to tell you to be careful. That's all. Don't believe the hype, don't believe the music, and whatever you do, don't believe the man."

"Thank you," I say. "I really appreciate it."

"Thing is," he says. "You smart. You'd'a figured it out eventually. Sooner rather than later, I'm sure. Just thought I'd save you a little time and maybe . . . you know . . . make it safer for you."

I nod. "Thanks."

"Tell you who far more dangerous and in a different way," he says. "His so-called manager or whatever the hell he supposed to be, Irvin Hunter. That bastard . . . *a manager. Shee-it.* He don't know nothin' about music or the entertainment industry. All he know about is crime, criminals, criminal enterprises. But he protected Trace like the little bitch he is when they's inside and now Trace feels like he owes him. You'd think ol' Trace takin' it up the naughty place for him while they's inside would be enough, but . . ."

I nod in a way meant to be encouraging, though it doesn't seem like he necessarily needs any encouragement to keep talking.

"Manager, Shee-it. Probably just uses him to carry his money around for him and sneak into his hotel room late at night."

"Whatta you mean carry his money around for him?"

"Trace is like a poor nigga's Floyd Mayweather," he says. "Money Mayweather, who isn't just nigger rich like Trace, carries a million dollars in cash in a hockey bag with him at all times. Word is Trace can't roll that deep, so he always carries two-hundred-and-fifty thousand on him. Figure that's Irvin's job. Carry that shit around. Rub his face in it."

I don't react outwardly, but inwardly I'm reeling. If Trace always keeps a quarter of a million dollars in cash on him at all times then the kidnaper chose that amount so Trace could pay in cash and not have to involve a bank.

"Is that common knowledge?" I ask.

"What?"

"How much money Trace carries with him in cash."

He shakes his head. "Not like it is with Mayweather. He doesn't flaunt it or talk about it like he does. You'd have to be a true fan who dives deep or a friend."

"You two still friends?" I ask.

"He still accepts my collect calls," he says.

Collect calls are the only kind inmates can make. And if he's telling the truth, then Trace is on his approved call list.

"How long since you've talked to him?"

He shrugs. "Last month sometime. He's pretty good to send me some canteen when I run out."

"That term you used," I say.

"What's that?" he asks. "Oh," he adds with a smile, "nigger rich?"

"I've heard it before and think I know what it means, but would you tell me what you think it means and why you used it about Trace?"

"Nigger rich is when you have just a little money and you spend on things that can be seen. Shiny new Cadillac, rims, gold teeth, gold chains, what not, but live in a dump or have no money in the bank. Spend it on flashy shit the minute you get it. I ain't sayin' Trace is just like that, but . . . I don't know. Just meant he's got a lot less than Floyd and . . . And he's got a song called Nigger Rich."

"Really?"

"Oh yeah. Hell, I helped him write it."

"So both Trace and Irvin Hunter are dangerous, but in different ways," I say.

He nods.

"Trace may've killed his kid, but Hunter will kill you," he says. "Keep your eyes on that nigga."

"Got it."

"Then they's one more player in this little drama you betta watch out for. Another nigga they used to run with—Little Swag."

"Rondarius Swaggart," I say.

"So you heard of him. Ain't sayin' he's a direct threat to you, just . . . They had a fallin' out or some shit. Wouldn't want you to get caught in the crossfire. You know how nigga's like to be shootin' each other. This shit develops into a Biggie Tupac situation, wouldn't want you to be some kind of cracker collateral damage."

29

"*Cracker collateral damage?*" Anna says.

"That's what he doesn't want me to become," I say.

"Me either," she says.

"Let's hope none of us become that," Reggie says.

It's evening. Reggie has stopped by on her way home. She and I are sitting at our kitchen table as Anna makes dinner a short distance away. The girls are intensely playing with a variety of toys in the corner of the living room where Sam's hospital bed used to be.

"You sure you won't stay and eat with us?" Anna says.

We had both already asked and both been told *no*.

"Keep askin'," she says. "Smells so good my resolve is weakening."

"It's settled," she says. "I'm gonna make you a plate too when it's done."

Reggie looks back at me. "Do you believe what the inmate said about Trace? Be very telling if he does carry two-hundred-and-fifty thousand dollars around with him at all times."

"Yes it would. I've asked around some. I think it's legit. Far as everything else Chance said . . . I believe some of it. Need confirmation for other parts of it. But I did leave my interview with Trace thinking he acted and sounded a little too good to be true."

She nods. "Yeah, things aren't adding up. Aren't what they seem. You heard all the stuff about him that's come out in the media?"

I shake my head. "Avoiding it completely."

"Probably a good thing, though I don't know how you're able to. It's everywhere. They're saying plenty of shit about our department too. And about you and me. Mentioned Robin's murder and how I got the job. Mentioned you working the Stone Cold Killer case back in the day."

"Don't tell me," I say. "I don't want to know."

"None of it?"

"None."

"I feel like we need to do a press conference soon," she says. "Not sure whether to just make a statement, try to correct all the misinformation, take questions. I was hoping you'd participate."

"I'd really rather not," I say. "I want to work this case with little to no contact with any media of any kind. And whoever does it—I think it needs to be you, they'd chew Arnie up and spit him out—trying to correct all the incorrect information is as futile as trying to clean up a hurricane with a hand towel."

She shakes her head and frowns. "Case like this has a life of its own out in the public sphere, doesn't it? Nothing we can do about it. And I get that it's a shocking and compelling mystery and that the public's appetite for information is insatiable, but the tabloid-type shit they're all reporting isn't just irresponsible, it's . . . dangerous . . . damaging . . . lies."

"Makes you wonder how much information out there on any subject is accurate, doesn't it?" Anna says.

"Part of the reason I don't want to go home right now," Reggie says, "is I can't talk about the case with Merrick and that's all he wants to talk about."

I nod and attempt to convey understanding.

"Not sure if we're gonna make it," she says. "And that's something I never thought I'd hear myself say. But . . . there's just so much conflict all of the time. Anyway . . . Didn't come here to talk about that. The real reason I dropped by was . . . Couple of things I found out today . . . Didn't want to wait 'til tomorrow to tell you."

"What's that?"

"All the keys to the rental house are accounted for. None are missing—not to the house or the secret room."

"This is from Justin Harris?" I ask.

"Yeah, but remember it makes him more of a suspect if it's true," she says. "So I don't think he's lying."

"If it's true," I say, "then he and the owner . . . Roger Garrett are supposed to be the only ones with keys besides the renters."

"Right. Narrows things down a lot."

"Except anyone—a maid, a previous renter, someone who works in Justin's office, a handyman—"

"Repair person," Anna corrects from the kitchen.

"Repair person," I amend. "Any of them could've made copies of the keys."

"That's the other thing," Reggie says. "They couldn't. They can't. Garrett put in this elaborate lock system where the keys are made with lasers and have a chip in them and cannot be copied."

"Really?"

"Uh huh."

"Of course someone paranoid enough to have a secret safe room would have keys you can't copy," Anna says. "So . . . since there was no break-in, it was either someone inside, Harris, Garrett?"

"Or," I say, "someone stayed inside after the party, or someone left a window or door unlocked or someone inside let someone from outside in."

In her best Alex Hunter, the DA in the JonBenét Ramsey case, Reggie says "The field of suspects narrows. Soon the only one on the list will be you."

I nod. "It does narrow the list down considerably."

"Think Merrill may have backed a losing horse," Reggie says.

"Why's that?"

"Not looking good for Trace," she says.

"Merrill's not backin' him," I say. "He'll be the first to take him down if he killed his little girl."

"Well that's what it's looking like," she says. "He or one of the people he had in the house with him."

30

That night with all three of my girls in the room with me, I worked on the case in the pale illumination of the small book light clipped to the murder book.

I think about what Reggie said about the media coverage, about Trace's public image, and can imagine what is being reported. I'm sure he and Ashley and Brett and Nadine and Irvin have already been found guilty in the minds of most passive, non-critical consumers of media. John and Patsy and Burke were. And though statistically the odds of a family member or someone in the house the night of the murders is very, very high, a likelihood is not a certainty.

Why are we so quick to believe the worst about certain people and not others? What is it about John and Patsy and Trace that make them so easy to despise, condemn, presume guilty?

Why are we so quick to listen to information that confirms our biases and reject that which challenges them?

Why did so many refuse to believe OJ was guilty in spite of concrete physical evidence?

I think about the keys being accounted for and not being able to be copied and what that might mean.

No forced entry. No missing keys. Six people in the house.

I think about the notes—the fact that Mariah planned to run away and her motivation for doing so, the fact that in spite of the runaway note, the kidnaper left the ransom note.

I think about the use of Trace's song lyrics in the note and the demand of the exact amount of cash he keeps with him at all times. Was the note part of staging to cover up the true crime of murder? Does it include so much inside information because someone inside the house and deep inside Trace's life wrote it—including or especially Trace himself?

I consider the ropes used to tie up Mariah, the fact that they belonged to Trace and Ashley and were used in his sexually suggestive music video.

Ashley and Brett or to mean to me. I love them but cannot take it.

The line from Mariah's runaway note floats through my mind. And with it another question.

Was the runaway note part of staging? Did Mariah even write it? If she did, was it from an earlier time, kept by someone and used to confuse this situation?

As usual, I have far more questions than answers, but the questions are instructive and may lead to some crucial answers.

I think about Mariah and JonBenét and ask the question that contains its own answer—Why is it always the most vulnerable among us who are victimized?

I think about how both little girls were tied up, sexually assaulted, and received a savage blow to the back of the head.

But whereas that appears to be the extent of what happened to Mariah—and even her sexual assault was from the day before —JonBenét was garroted, suffered a far more horrific death, her body bearing not only the marks of brutality and violence, but the defensive wounds of fingernails scratching her own neck as she fought against the garrote that was choking the life from her little body.

Suddenly I am overwhelmed with grief and fear, thinking

about unthinkable things as I listen to the sweet sounds of Johanna and Taylor's breathing.

I'm stricken with stifling heart-breaking heaviness for Mariah and JonBenét and filled with a dreadful fear for Johanna and Taylor.

Why did Mariah and JonBenét have to suffer such horrific deaths? Why'd they have to die at all?

Will I be able to protect Johanna and Taylor? How about when I'm not around? What happens to them if something happens to me?

As if a powerful constricting serpent, fear coils around my heart and lungs and I feel as if I'm dying.

Can't breathe.

Can't . . . feel my . . . pulse.

Though there is so much more I need to be studying and thinking about, I click off the light, place the murder book on the floor, and slide over to hold Anna and feel her warmth, her life, her heartbeat.

"Hey," she whispers. "You okay?"

She shimmies into me, contouring her body to mine, her warmth and life and heartbeat immediately beginning to comfort and heal and revive.

I nod. "Will be. Just needed to feel you, your life."

She reaches around behind her and pulls me to her even more.

"First case like this since we've had the girls," I say. "Not sure I can do it."

She pulls me even tighter with her left hand and squeezes my hand with her right, and by not saying anything lets me know she not only understands but will love me no less no matter what I do —even if I can no longer do one of the things so core to me, so essential to who I am, that I can't remember not doing it, can't remember not being it.

31

I wake up feeling much better, which may have something to do with waking up in Anna'a arms and having both girls in bed with us.

By the time I'm showered and dressed, the smell of breakfast is wafting through our big old house.

When I reach the kitchen, Anna is placing breakfast on the table and Reggie is sitting down to it, Johanna catty-cornered across from her on a stool at the table, Taylor at the end in her highchair.

"Morning," I say to Reggie.

"Morning," she says. "Dinner was so good I came back for breakfast."

"*Morning, beautiful*," I say to Anna and kiss her before taking a seat across from Reggie.

"Morning ladies," I say to Johanna and Taylor, and kiss Johanna, who is next to me, on the head.

"I'm coming," Anna says, "but y'all go ahead and start. Don't let it get cold."

"It's not gonna get cold," I say, "but even if it does, I'm waiting on you."

"I'm not," Reggie says, and begins to dip the white sausage gravy onto the huge cathead biscuit on her plate.

In her highchair, Taylor is eating some sort of mushy, soft cereal, and next to me at the table, Johanna is pinching small bites of biscuit, the crunchy golden crust on the top, with her thumb and index finger.

"Would you open this for me, Daddy?" Johanna asks, lifting the large jar of jelly with her little hands and passing it to me, her biscuit-greasy fingertips leaving a little residue on the moist jar.

"Gladly," I say.

Anna joins us and we all begin or continue to eat.

Before we've eaten much, there's a knock on the door.

"I've got it," I say, jumping up and dashing over to the door.

When I open the door, Sam and Daniel are standing there backlit by the morning sun.

"We were out for our morning constitutional," Daniel says, "and smelled breakfast."

"Come in. Come in. You're just in time."

By the time we reach the table, Anna has two more plates and is fixing them.

I grab an extra stool from the garage, and in a few minutes we're all breaking bread together in a way that nourishes far more than just our bodies.

"We miss you, Ms. Sam," Johanna says. "When are you coming back?"

"I . . . miss . . . y'all . . . too," she says.

As good as the breakfast is and as appetizing as it smells, I know it's not the real reason Reggie is here, and I suspect Daniel and Sam are here not because they smelled it, but because Anna invited them.

Reggie looks at Daniel. "When you gonna help Merrick with the podcast again? He's struggling without you. Needs you back."

He shrugs. "Not quite ready yet. But getting there."

As he eats, I can see the outline of the weapon beneath his

shirttails on this side. Reggie helped him get a concealed carry permit when he and Sam moved out of our place into their own. And though he didn't say so, I know it's because of his recent experiences with Randa Rafffield.

The biscuits are big and dense, the sausage gravy creamy and spicy, and I eat more, and more quickly, than I should.

Eventually, I say to Reggie, "You might as well say what you came here to say in front of them. Not only can you trust them, but I'm going to tell them anyway."

She smiles. "I was going to. Was just finishing my breakfast first."

"Any ... thing ... coming from the ... search of known ... sex offenders in the ... area?" Sam asks.

Reggie shakes her head. "Nothin' so far from the ones we know about, the ones that are actually registered and were in the area that night. But I'm wondering how many there are we don't know about—who're either not registered or were in the area without us knowing."

Sam nods.

"Not gettin' any joy from the list of previous renters or cleaning staff either," she says. "House like that ... doesn't rent much, so the list was small and so far it seems everybody has an ironclad alibi. We'll know more when we start getting some DNA results back, but at this point it really looks like it was someone staying in the house—Trace or Ashley or Irvin."

"But none of that's why you stopped by," I said, "any more than breakfast is."

She smiles and nods. "True. Got some results on the ransom note first thing this morning. Lab's in Tallahassee and an hour ahead of us. Didn't realize how early he was calling. I told him to always call as early as he possibly can. So ... we don't have any handwriting results yet, and we'll really need them to know what we need to know, but ... the pen used to write the ransom note was in the house. They got a match to a cheap promo pen in one of the kitchen drawers with a Justin Harris Real Estate logo on it."

Anna says, "So far all the evidence is pointing in the same direction."

"How about the paper it was written on?" I say. "Did it—"

"That's the best part," she says. "It's a sheet of paper ripped out of Trace Evers' songwriting journal—the one he never goes anywhere without, the one that is never very far away from him at any time."

32

After graduating high school and a tearful goodbye at which my mom smelled of booze and from which my dad was absent, I had loaded my car, filled my tank using some of my graduation money, and set out for the city too busy to hate.

A little over three decades later, I'm heading back to Atlanta again.

Atlanta is haunted for me, sure, but it's also a reservoir of experiences and memories that seem somehow to be touched with magic, and I feel a unique connection to this place that is the birthplace of my hero and spiritual mentor Martin Luther King, Jr.

I can't help but love Atlanta, and returning, even alone and under these circumstances brings a certain type of homesick satisfaction that I don't experience visiting any other place on the planet.

It had been extremely difficult leaving Anna and the girls, but there was no scenario we could come up with that would make this work trip anything but miserable for them if they came with me.

Before leaving, I had set up security for them, which with Merrill in Atlanta with Trace, had been challenging.

Ironically, what wound up working best was Daniel and Sam moving back into the place they had just moved out of. Dad and Jake were also helping—taking shifts when Daniel slept or had to be away. I also had deputies driving by regularly, conspicuously making their presence known. With Chris so close and Randa still on the loose, I wouldn't have agreed to leave any other way.

My first stop in Atlanta is Myra House.

Located in South Dekalb where I had spent so much time in my youth, pursuing that which I had felt pursued for—murder investigation and ministry, Myra House is a home for battered and drug-addicted women named after Mariah's mother, Myra Baxley.

Situated at the bottom of a severe slope just off Wesley Chapel Road, Myra House is a sprawling old partially remodeled split-level ranch surrounded by a high chain-link fence and fronted by a guard at a gate.

And though I'm expected and a law enforcement officer, I have difficulty getting in, the overzealous gate guard reminding me of Ralph Alderman, the security guard at Safe Haven, Miss Ida's daycare, which was less than two miles from here.

"Sorry about that," Deidre says. "We can't be too careful. I know it's a hassle, but it saves lives."

We are standing near where I have just parked my car in what once was the side yard of this home.

Deidre Baxley, Myra's sister and Mariah's aunt, is a small, attractive dark-haired woman who could be beautiful if not for the grief and exhaustion.

"I completely understand," I say. "And appreciate it. Is the biggest threat from abusive husbands or drug dealers or . . ."

"Lot of people don't like what we're doing," she says. "For a lot of different reasons. Not just the obvious victimizers who feel like they own the victims who live here. Even our neighbors don't want us here."

"Really? Why?"

"They're not against helping victims of domestic violence and addicts," she says. "They just don't want us to do it here. Chain link and razor wire and men trying to break in and bullets flying about aren't exactly good for property values, but let's get inside. Not a good idea to stand out here like this."

"Even way back here?" I say. "Why's that?"

"We've had a number of drive-bys," she says. "Some of the shots hit back here. Look at that tree."

I follow her glance over to an oak tree with bullet holes in it.

She leads me inside, where I am eyed warily by every woman I encounter.

In what appears to be the main rec room, a handful of women, black and white, young and middle-aged, sit on worn and mismatched furniture watching an afternoon talkshow.

We continue through the house, down hallways and up stairs, the smell I associate with older, inexpensive hotels.

Through the large dining room where two teens who look like girls far too young to be in a place like this are setting the extremely long table and into the kitchen where older women in hairnets and aprons appear to be preparing the evening meal.

Down another long hallway, this one with bedroom doors off to each side.

Finally we arrive at Deidra's office.

"Come in and have a seat," she says.

The office is small, clean but cluttered, and smells better than the rest of the house.

Framed photographs, tacked up posters and bumper stickers, hand-painted signs, all bear similar themed slogans: *You Hit, We Hurt. A house where a woman is not safe is not a home. A Slap is not a Solution. End the Silence of Domestic Violence. The scars you can't see are the hardest to heal.*

"I'm so sorry about your niece," I say.

Her sad, weary eyes become even more sad and tired and I can see tears forming.

"Thank you," she says. "It . . . it feels so familiar—and not just because of what he did to her mother, but because of what he did to her where we were concerned. We've grieving the loss of Mariah almost as long as Myra. He took them both from us. Twice. Myra with domination, control, drugs, alcohol, and eventually death. Mariah with sole custody, control, domination, and eventually death. God, I feel like I should've used all my tears by now."

She wipes at the tears creasing the corners of her eyes.

I wait, resisting the urge to speak.

We are quiet for a short while.

From down the hall I can hear women talking. Not unsurprisingly no laughter accompanies their interaction.

"You're not like any cop I've ever seen," she says. "Seem more like a counselor."

"I do some of that too," I say. "My other car's chaplaincy."

She looks confused at first, but then nods her head as she gets it.

"I'm well acquainted with loss and grief," I say.

"Not just professionally, I take it," she says.

I nod. "Lost two people extremely close to me not two miles from here when I was very young," I say.

"Never get over it, do you?"

I shake my head. "Not ever."

"I miss Myra every day," she says. "Every single day. Mariah wasn't really a part of our lives—Trace saw to that—but I already feel the loss of her. And that's just on a selfish level—me thinking about how much I'm gonna miss her—which is nothing compared to the horror of thinking of what was done to her or the despair of realizing that sweet child doesn't get to grow up and become who she might have been—to fall in love, to have a child, to use her talents. It's . . . overwhelming to even consider."

I wait.

"Oh, I guess I should've said it first and gotten it out of the way—I know y'all look at everybody especially the family—including the family that's not even in her life, but I took my parents to the North Georgia Mountains for the holiday. I'm all they have now since Trace took Myra from them and they're getting older and I spend so much of my time here . . . it was a nice little getaway. We were at the Red Roof Inn in Helen, Georgia if you want to look into it. We were there for three days. I had to come back here for a few hours of the second day. Had an employee who got drunk and didn't show up for her shift and a new intake, but then I drove back up and . . . we were there when we got the news about Mariah. It's interesting. We drove straight back right then though it didn't happen here and she wasn't here and wouldn't be for some time, but . . . it's like we just had to be home. Couldn't be on vacation after what happened."

I nod. "I get that."

"Can't believe I didn't get to be in her life more," she says. "That's the thing. Her whole life is over. She's not getting any more. Not another breath. Not another heartbeat. Not another hug. Not another smile. Not another laugh. I missed it. Missed so much."

"Trace kept you from her?"

She nods. "Kept her from me and my parents," she says.

"Why?"

She frowns and seems to think about it. "Not just one reason. He has to control everything—his image, his women, his posse, his children. But mostly it's because he knows we know he killed Myra. He beat her and got her strung out on alcohol and drugs and then he killed her."

"Are you saying he contributed to her death or that he actually murdered her?" I ask.

"I know you're not asking a sister to make a distinction like that," she says.

"Sorry," I say. "You're right. I was just trying to get a picture of Trace and their relationship, and what happened."

"You want to know who Trace is?" she says. "Look at OJ. I'm talkin' about back when he was younger, not shot out and crazy like he is now. Controlling. Jealous. Abusive. He didn't murder her with a knife like OJ did, but he didn't kill her any less than OJ killed Nicole. Nicole's death was more violent, but death by overdose is just as dead."

I nod.

"Have you met him?" she asks.

I nod again.

"Bet he impressed you, didn't he? Said all the right things. Seems like essentially a good person. He's a sociopath. A master manipulator."

I nod again because I can't think of anything else to do and I don't want to stop her flow.

"I remember my poor sister reading books about bondage and being a bottom, trying to learn how to be submissive and be tied up. She actually practiced. It was so sad. It wasn't natural to her. I know plenty of women—and men for that matter who like to be tied up—so it's not that. It's that it wasn't her thing, that he wouldn't find her thing. It had to be what he wanted. She had to conform and contort and eventually lose herself by trying to transform into what he wanted. Makes me sick to my stomach just to think about."

I try to think of something to do beside nod, but am unable to come up with anything.

"You going to her funeral tomorrow?" she asks.

"I am."

"My parents and I would love to be there, but we can't," she says. "Can you imagine? Nowhere her grandparents would rather be than at her funeral and they can't go. Best case scenario would be if his thugs just kept us from going in, but there's every chance my aging parents, truly decent people, would be assaulted or worse."

"Would you like for me to talk to Trace or the Atlanta authorities?" I say. "See if I can work it out so y'all can go?"

Tears fill her eyes again. "That's . . . very gracious of you. It means a lot that you would even try. But there's no way he'd go for anything like that. He hated us before we started Myra House, but afterward . . . he wants us dead. I took every dime of life insurance Myra had and started this home in her honor to stop other women from becoming victims like her. Not only did he want the money for himself, he certainly didn't want a place like this named after the woman he beat and shot up and killed. And we've been open about Myra's story, so everyone who comes through these doors or reads about us in the press or online knows what he did to her, who he really is."

"This is such an incredible thing to do for her, for her legacy," I say. "You said how decent your parents are . . . clearly you are too."

She shakes her head. "I'm . . . just a sad person with no life. Since I didn't plan on living anymore anyway, why not try to let Myra's life and death give life and hope to others."

"It's truly inspiring."

"Be inspired by the survivors who come here," she says. "Who leave here and never go back to an abusive relationship or a needle or pipe. They're inspiring. I'm just the half-dead-inside, too-early-old little mouse who pays the bills around here. The only little bit of light I've had in my life for the last few years is the tiny little bit of Mariah I got—a text or email or Snapchat. They were rare—she had to sneak to do even those, but . . . I lived for them, for some small part of Myra to show through her daughter's eyes or in her smile . . . and now I don't even have that."

I feel so sorry for this smart, self-aware, too-early-old, grief-stricken young woman before me, but know there's nothing I can say or do that would be of much comfort or use to her.

"I'm so very sorry," I say—because there is nothing else to say.

"She . . . was such a ray of sunshine," she continues, as if I hadn't spoken. "Such a free spirit, so loving and . . . man did she know how to have fun. Like I say, I saw her very, very little, but the few times I did was like being around a radiant light that made you radiate with it long afterwards."

"How would you see her?" I ask. "Where?"

"She'd text me and say she was with a friend at the mall or the movies, and I'd meet her there for a few minutes—usually in the bathroom or somewhere like that. We're only talking a handful of times over the past couple of years. I was able to take my folks twice. Made their life."

"I'm so glad y'all got that," I say.

"That reminds me . . .Mom gave her a pair of earrings—Trace wouldn't let her get her ears pierced yet, so Mom bought her a pair of clip-ons and gave them to her the last time we saw her. And I gave her a frame I had made of pictures of me and her mom when we were girls and then the two of us with her when she was born. If there's any way to get them back . . . I know she had to hide them from Trace . . . so I have no idea where they might be—though one time she did tell me she carried them everywhere she went. Anyway, I'd really like to get them back if at all possible. The thought of him having them or destroying them . . ."

I nod. "I'll see what I can do."

"Thank you."

"Who do you think killed Mariah?" I ask.

She frowns. "I don't think. I know. It was Trace. No question."

"You don't think it was Ashley or anyone else in the house that night?"

She shakes her head. "I'd bet my life it was Trace and that it was about control," she says. "They're saying that there was a note saying she was going to run away. If so, if she'd had enough and was going to get out from underneath his oppressive control . . . all that would have had to happen was him finding out about it and him losing his temper as he imposed his will on her. I wouldn't call that an accident, but her death could have been unintentional. But death is death. Murder is murder. He did it. It's on him. He's to blame. You said you were getting fingerprints and handwriting samples from everyone. Well, my mom and dad and I would be happy to provide them because the quicker you can eliminate everyone else, the better. So you can focus on him. He did it. No doubt in my mind. Like I said, I'd bet my life on it."

33

"I'm a bottom," Ashley Howard says. "Trace is a top. It's why we fit so well together. Are you familiar with those terms?"

Like Trace, Ashely continues to talk openly and freely with me, seemingly without second guessing or editing herself.

I nod. "Yes, but I'd appreciate hearing how you describe them."

We are in a large formal living room inside Trace's enormous and exquisite mansion, sitting in high back leather chairs with a view of Trace's stable of exotic sports cars—most of which I had never even heard of.

The house and everything in it and the cars make me think Trace is extremely overextended. There's no way he has built up the kind of wealth required for this kind of lifestyle over his relatively short career, and it reminds me of how the ransom note referred to him.

Trace is at the funeral home. Merrill is with him. I hope to still be here when they get back.

Above the large fireplace a huge painted portrait of Mariah hangs in a frame that might actually be made of gold. In it, her genuine smile makes her eyes sparkle and adds an effervescent quality to her flawless face.

I notice there are no pictures of Ashley or Brett in the room.

"Sure. They're like the roles we play. A bottom is the submissive, the one who is tied up, dominated, told what to do. The top is the one who does the tying, the one who dominates, who gives the order, who's in control. Trace is a top. I'm a bottom."

"Do you ever switch roles?" I ask.

She shakes her head. "Not in the bedroom, no. I think that may have been the problem with his first wife. She wanted to be a top and a bottom. You can't really be both. I know some people say they switch, but I don't see how you can. Trace is an excellent top. In command. In control. No one has ever given me the pleasure he has. Not in my entire life. I couldn't do that. Not what he does. I give him pleasure by submitting to him, by doing exactly what he tells me to. No more and no less. I love being tied up. It's freeing for me. I'm sure he would find it . . . it would feel like shackles to him."

"Do you always travel with your ropes and kit?" I ask.

She nods emphatically. "Always. We're insatiable. That's another thing that makes us work so well together. We both love sex. Both love our roles in our sex. I do what he tells me when he tells me. He can say drop to your knees and go down on me anywhere at any time and I do. One of the games we play is having sex is as many different places as possible, places where we might get caught, place where other people are—like in the backseat of a cab or under the table at a restaurant, that sort of thing. But mostly we just have a lot of sex. And love it. I don't understand people who don't love sex and get as much of it as they can. But to each his own, right? Why do you think we have a nanny? I need help with the kids so I can be a good bottom. So I can be at his beck and call."

From what I've been told, we've so far been able to keep the details about the ropes used on Mariah out of the press, but since

Trace had to have seen them when he pulled Mariah's body from beneath her bed, I would have thought he would have told Ashley about them. Of course, if he or she or they used them on Mariah, they'd know about them anyway. Whatever the case, I'd expect her to mention the significance of the ropes in the light of the case, but she's not. So far, she's answering my questions as if they're the casual inquiries of someone either interested in trying bondage or curious about her sex life. It's an odd disconnect that I find jarring.

"Are y'all monogamous?" I ask.

"Sort of."

"How can you be sort of monogamous?"

"Half and half," she says. "I am. He's not. I can't keep up with him. He's . . ." She shakes her head "He's a force. Unstoppable, unmatchable."

"You okay with him not being monogamous?"

"He's the top. I'm the bottom. He tells me I can't be, but he can. That's what goes. He owns me. I am his body and soul. And by giving him what he wants . . . by letting him be free . . . he always comes back to me. Nobody out there will give him what I do, will be for him what I am."

I can't help but notice she never really did answer my question.

"All this because you found our ropes and toys in our luggage?" she says.

Is she pretending not to know the actual significance of my questions in relationship to the ropes and Mariah's murder or does she really not know?

"Just being thorough," I say.

"Well, you're not asking about the other things in our luggage," she says.

"Different investigators are focusing on different aspects of the case."

"And you got my sex life," she says.

"I got ropes."

"Okay," she says. "Just seems a little . . . I don't know . . . off subject. How's this going to help you find who did this to Mariah?"

"That's the thing about an investigation," I say. "You never know what is and isn't on or off subject. We have to gather mountains of information, sift through it, and see what, if any, patterns or connections emerge."

"Well, Trace says you know what you're doing—at least according to Merrill, but . . . it seems . . . I don't know. Just want Mariah's killer found. Not that it will bring her back or anything, but . . ."

I nod.

"Seems like more and more cases don't get solved," she says. "Is that true?"

"It is."

"I hope Mariah's won't be one of them. Bad enough to lose a child, but to not know who took them from you or why . . . I'm not sure Trace is going to survive this. Not sure we are."

Before I can respond, Brett drifts into the room, his head down, his attention focused on the handheld gaming device he's gripping.

"Hey baby boy," Ashley says to Brett, then to me, "I don't see how he doesn't walk into things trying to walk and play that thing at the same time, but he never does."

As if on cue, he bumps into the coffee table.

"You just made Mommy a liar," she says.

"Sorry."

He joins her on the couch, sitting right up against and leaning on her, never looking up from his game.

"You missing Mariah?" she says.

He shrugs.

"Bored without someone to play with?"

"Glad . . . I don't have . . . to share anymore."

Every word comes between the pressing and tapping of buttons.

"But you loved Mariah," she says. "Loved playing with her."

He doesn't respond.

"Brett," she says, "don't you miss Mariah? Aren't you sorry she's gone?"

He shrugs. "I ... get more now."

Ashley looks at me, her eyes searching mine for judgement.

"More what?" she asks him.

"I don't know ... Everything. She got all the ... candy and ... presents ... and ... attention."

"Yeah, but you're going to miss her, aren't you?"

He doesn't respond.

"Brett," she says, her voice growing stern. "Answer Mommy. You're going to miss Mariah, aren't you?"

"Yes, ma'am," he says without conviction or sincerity.

"He will," she says, looking back at me. "Just hasn't sunk in yet. You know how kids are. Almost as self-centered as Trace is."

34

"I was the closest thing to a mother that child ever had," Nadine says. "I loved her like a daughter. Still can't believe she's really gone."

"I'm so sorry for your loss," I say.

"World's a colder, lonelier place now," she says. "Least for me. Raised her like she was my own."

Nadine Wade is old enough to be Mariah's grandmother, but looks like she could be her mother. Her dark skin shows no wrinkles or aging marks, her narrow frame and lean body looking like that of a thirty-something instead of the fifty-something she is. She has no discernible makeup on and is actually wearing what looks to be a gray maid's uniform. Her closely cropped hair looks like a style invented for someone who cares far more about convenience than appearance.

I am sitting with her in a sunroom on the side of the house that leads out to the pool. It's far warmer in the room than is comfortable for me, but Nadine seems to like it.

"Nobody understands," she says. "Nobody lettin' me grieve like a mother. Nobody tryin' to help or comfort me or . . . nothin'. Trace should know better. But I know he's too torn up inside to be thinkin' of anyone but himself right now. And that damn dumb white trash nympho . . . actin' like she cared for the child at all. Makes me so mad, I want to crush her skull."

I think about all those unsung, unofficial sufferers in the world—secret lovers, caregivers, nannies, hidden friends—who are forced to mourn alone, unacknowledged, uncomforted, unknown to official family members. I think this used to be particularly true in gay relationships, though I hope that is changing.

"That little angel was all I had in this world. All."

I nod, but don't say anything.

Like the rest of the house, the sunroom looks to have been professionally decorated by someone with a big budget told that when they think they've gone too gaudy and ostentatious, go a little more. Much of what's in here clashes and though it looks like it cost a lot of money, it looks like that was the only goal.

Nadine notices me looking around the room.

"All this," she says, stretching her hand out like a gameshow assistant. "Can't protect you when a thief comes knocking. Grim Reaper don't care what your address is or how big or small your house is, does he?"

"He does not," I say.

"I've turned in my notice," she says. "Can't work here anymore. Not just to keep . . . *her* kid. Don't need a nanny for him no way, just a video game."

"How did he and Mariah get along?" I ask.

She shakes her head. "Didn't interact much. She'd try to get him to play or watch her perform or something, do some typical kid stuff, but all he wanted to do was play that blasted video game. Wasn't studying nothing but clicking buttons. When he would decide to play with her, they had to do what he wanted to do. She was a pretty good sport."

Tears begin streaming from her eyes and she wipes them with small, crumpled tissues.

"I just can't believe . . ."

"Who could've done something like this?" I ask.

She shakes her head. "Can't fathom it. No earthly idea how any human being could do that to a precious child. Nobody I know. Nobody human."

"Nobody you know?" I ask. "Nobody who was on vacation with y'all?"

"No way. Them folks got their issues like anybody else—more than most maybe, but . . . do something like that . . . no way."

"So you think somehow somebody got in the house and . . ."

"A sure enough monster of a man got in that house," she says. "No other explanation."

"How about an accident?" I say. "Then a cover-up?"

She shakes her head emphatically. "Accident, sure" she says. "Accident can happen, but not all that other stuff. Ransom note and tying the poor thing up and shoving her under her bed like that. None of them could've done all that. Accident happens, we call an ambulance. Simple as that."

I nod.

We are quiet a beat.

"Did Mariah take her iPod with her on this trip?"

She lets out a little laugh. "She didn't go to the next room without it. Was like the thing was surgically attached to her hand. Always tap-tap-tappin' on it. Her daddy wouldn't let her have a phone, but might as well have. She talked to everybody. Tap, tap, tap."

"Did something happen to it while y'all were there?" I ask. "It wasn't with her things?"

She shakes her head. "She had it when I put her to bed . . . that . . . night."

"Can you think of what might have happened to it?"

"Well . . . Brett wanted one. Was always after his mama to get him one, but she said that game device was enough. Said if she ever got him a second device he'd never ever look up. He was always askin' her to borrow it. What they fought over mostly. He could've . . . If he didn't take it . . . suppose her killer could have, but . . . why would he steal her iPod? Did he take anything else?"

"Not that we know of."

"Hmm," she says, and narrows her eyes and twists her lips in thought.

"Anything happen out of the ordinary during the vacation?" I ask.

"Not especially, no."

"Anybody at the party act suspicious or—"

"Not that I saw, but I wasn't around much. Took the kids upstairs pretty early and let them play."

"Caden Stevens was there too, right?"

She nods. "He and Mariah were sweet on each other," she says. "He hadn't seen her video. Didn't know or care who her daddy was. Just liked her for her. She liked him too. Made Master Brett *jeal-ous*. Decided he wanted to play with her then, but it was too late."

"Did he do anything, act out in any way?"

She shakes her head. "Nah. And I kept a pretty close eye on all them. Caught Caden and Mariah kissin'. Wanted to make sure they didn't do anything else. Kept going in her room, made 'em keep the door open. Every time I checked on them, Brett wasn't even in there with them. He was in his room playin' that damn computer game thing."

"Any adults come up there that night?" I ask. "Wander up from the party?"

"A few. Say they want to check out the house. Can't remember all of them. Some of Trace's Atlanta friends and Ashley's obnoxious family I think. And Irvin and Justin. I thought that was odd, 'cause they both been up and was very familiar with the house. Justin especially. He rents it, you know. Made me think he was checking up on us, making sure we were treating his property properly. But I don't know. He talked to the kids a little while.

Mostly stayed in Brett's room with him. Probably thought the poor fella was being left out and felt sorry for him. Like I say, it was strange."

"Did you hear anything the night of the . . . the night Mariah was killed? Anything out of the ordinary?"

"No. Would've gotten up and checked on it if I had."

"Did you hear the elevator being used that night?"

She shrugs. "Think so, but can't be sure."

"Do you know about what time?"

"No idea. And maybe I didn't. Don't know for sure. Tell you what I do know . . . I think maybe I was drugged."

"Why's that?"

"I can't recall a single night in my entire adult life where I slept all the way through the night. And I don't even remember stirring. I fell asleep early, slept in later than usual, and slept hard as I can ever remember. Was like I was in coma. No tellin' what all went on in that house that night. Whatever it was, I wasn't conscious for it."

35

"I'll answer all the questions you have," Trace says, "but just answer one for me first."

"Okay."

"Are you really looking for my little girl's killer or are you just trying to build a case against me?"

We are in his music room in the back of the house.

The enormous room is filled with comfortable, expensive furniture and musical instruments, the walls covered with album cover art work, framed newspaper clippings, TV, film, and concert posters, framed publicity and live action photographs—the latter from concert stages and recording studios.

"I'm looking as hard as I can," I say. "Gathering evidence and information. Not building a case. Not yet. Not against you or anyone else. Just searching for the truth, looking for the killer, whoever he or she may be."

"Merrill says you're a prison chaplain too."

I nod.

"Can you tell me why God let this happen to my little girl?"

I shake my head. "I can't. I'm sorry."

"Hope you're a better cop than a chaplain."

I nod.

He studies me for a long moment. "You got no words of comfort for me?"

"Do you think any words exist that could be of comfort for what you're going through?"

"No. Guess not."

He seems to think about that for a long moment.

In addition to his own career memorabilia, autographed pictures and album covers of other rappers hang around the room—rappers so a part of the general, wider popular culture that I recognize many of them.

"Huh," he says. "You're right. They ain't invented words for shit like this. Might as well go ahead and ask your questions. You can't comfort me, least you can do is find the fuck who took my daughter from me."

"How did you sleep the night Mariah was killed?"

He shakes his head. "Wish I hadn't. Wish to God I hadn't. But . . . the best I have in years."

"Why do you think?"

"Didn't sleep much the night before. Too much liquor. Too much sun and beach and shit, I guess. Why?"

"Could you have been drugged?"

Tears fill his eyes. "I hope to Christ I was. Would make me feel a hell of a lot better if . . . if I wasn't just enjoying a nice night's sleep when my little girl was being strangled and assaulted and murdered."

His use of the word *strangled* stands out to me. Does he really not know how she died or is he being intentionally obtuse to appear innocent?

"I know this is extremely difficult, but . . . what do you remember about Mariah when you found her and pulled her out from beneath the bed?"

He blinks back tears and gets a hard look on his face. Fixing his eyes on something I can't see, he says, "How cold her skin was. How stiff her body was."

"What else?"

He narrows his eyes and furrows his brow in thought, them grimaces, as if the thoughts seem to cause him physical pain.

"Her eyes were open," he says. "I think she was tied up . . . but . . . a blanket was covering her."

"How did she look before you pulled her out?" I ask.

"Like she was sleeping under her bed the way she did when she was little."

"What about the blanket?"

"What about it?"

"Was it laid over her? Was she wrapped in it?"

"Completely wrapped. Like when she was a baby. Used to call her my little burrito."

"Was her face covered?"

"Yes."

"Are you sure? You said it looked like she was sleeping."

"No, wait. You're right. She . . . It wasn't."

"Did you write any songs while you were at the Cape?"

He seems to think about it, then shakes his head. "Intended to, but . . . didn't get around to it before . . ."

"Where did you keep your song journal?" I ask.

"Beside my bed like always. Why?"

"Did you move it at any time? Open it?"

"No," he says. "Why?"

"Just trying to—"

"You've got a reason for asking," he says. "What is it?"

"I know it's frustrating," I say, "but I can't answer any more questions right now. I can only ask them. Please believe me. All I'm trying to do is find who killed Mariah. I have no other agenda."

He nods and frowns.

"Someone said they read online that you always carry a quarter of a million dollars in cash," I say. "Is that true?"

He nods. "It's true, but I don't think it's online. Figured that's why the ransom note requested that amount."

"If it's not online, how many people would know about it?"

His eyes widen. "Not many. Ashley. Irvin. Nadine. Maybe a few close friends. Security. Not many. Unless it got online somehow, but . . . if it did . . . it'd have to be one of them to put in on there. But I don't think it's there. Who said it was?"

"Do you mind if I attend the funeral tomorrow?" I ask.

He shakes his head. "Not at all. Figured that's why you were in town."

"How about Mariah's grandparents and her aunt on her mother's side? Do you have any objections to them being there?"

"Not as long as they don't cause a scene. Tomorrow's too important for them to make it about them. I don't want to hear any talk about me killin' their daughter or granddaughter 'cause I didn't do either. I mean it. I don't want them to ruin our last chance to honor Mariah. Can you have police or security with them to shut that shit down if they start it? If you can assure me they won't cause a scene . . . I've got no problem with it."

I nod. "I'll see what I can do."

"I'm assuming you've already talked to them if they told you they want to come to the funeral. That because you're trying to gather dirt on me?"

I shake my head.

"You tryin' to set me up?" he says "Why else talk to them? Thought you were running a real investigation, not a witch hunt."

36

"Wonder what he's playing at?" Deidra says.

I've just told her Trace said she and her parents could attend the funeral if she could assure me no one would cause a scene.

"It's so funny he'd talk about us causing a scene—that's what I mean about him. He often says the opposite of what's really true. It's surreal. He's confronted us, yelled at us, caused any number of scenes in some very public and inappropriate places, but we never have and never would. Our family is not the make-a-scene kind of people. My parents are very reserved. Just makes me wonder what he's up to. Guess it doesn't matter as long as we get to be there for Mariah—unless he plans to use it to hurt or injure my folks in some way. I know. I know. It sounds paranoid, but I promise it's not. Anyway, thank you. Thank you so much for making this possible. I feel like I need to do something for you."

"Not at all. I just asked."

"At least let me take you to dinner tonight," she says. "Once a week, I take a different one of the Myra House women out to dinner. Try to get them out of the house, back used to living a little. . . some sense of normalcy. That sort of thing. Sandy, the young woman I'm taking tonight requested we go for a late dinner at Landmark Diner. She wants a juicy cheeseburger and the biggest slice of coconut cake in the metro area. Do you have plans? Would you like you join us?"

I consider what a night in a lonely hotel room with a minibar might do to both my sobriety and my mental state.

"I'd love to," I say. "Mind if I bring a friend?"

"Of course not. The more the merrier."

In the late afternoon, early evening, I locate and attend a meeting, visit with the Paulks, drop in and check on Miss Ida, call and setup my plus one for dinner tonight, go to Jordan's and Martin's graves, leaving flowers at Jordan's and a basketball at Martin's, marvel at both the city's explosive growth and extraordinary change, drive by a few of the places that hold good memories and no haunts for me, and call and check in with Anna and the girls. Then, on a last minute whim when I realized how close I was, visited the grave of JonBenét.

And then, after all of that, with some extra time on my hands that I didn't want to spend alone in the hotel room, I drive.

And drive.

And drive.

As the last of the light fades from the summer sky and the million billion city lights blink on below, as the traffic thins, in the midst of white and blue headlights and glowing red brake lights, I drive around the perimeter and through downtown streets.

Driving and thinking. Thinking and driving. Missing and mourning, feeling the bittersweet homesickness this city inspires in me, feeling nostalgic for what was for only the briefest of moments and will never be again.

Atlanta Nocturne.

Soft piano on the FM.

A trippy, atmospheric reinterpreting of *Claire de Lune*.

The city at night and I'm navigating its dark streets.

My head is filled with images, my ears ringing with information—playing basketball on the outdoor courts at Trade Winds with little Martin Fisher, finding Nicole Caldwell's dead body in my chapel office, Mariah Evers singing and dancing with her dad in the music video for *Never Leave You Again*, JonBenét in an elaborate pink and white ruffled costume complete with white cowboy hat and boots performing *I Want to Be a Cowboy's Sweetheart*, as snatches of conversation from today form a single continuous conversation.

Avoiding certain haunted places, like Memorial Drive, Flat Shoals Parkway, Stone Mountain, I speed through the city in what seems like slow motion, making my way to the Landmark Diner.

The streetlight-dotted night, the empty town, the skyline in the distance combine with the frame of mind I'm in to create a familiar mesmeric quality.

I'm reminded of the hypnotic ride I took with Summer Grantham after one of our meetings about the Atlanta Child Murders in the late 80's. We were in her Ted Bundy Bug and our ride through Atlanta at night was as hypnotic as she was.

My dinner date for tonight is Frank Morgan, the GBI agent and friend of my father's, who cared for me like a father when I lived here, taught me about being an investigator and a man, and saved my life more than once and in more ways than one.

Frank had recently lost his wife of nearly fifty years and I thought this little late-night outing might do him good.

He's waiting for me out front when I arrive.

The Landmark Diner is brightly lit, its neon-outlined exterior a beacon against the black night sky. The Greek-influenced, New

York-style diner, which opened in 1994, is open twenty-four hours a day, and is my favorite late-night eatery in the city.

As I walk up to it after parking on the side I recall bringing Susan here at midnight on the start of her birthday, celebrating her being in the world with lamb chops and chocolate cake.

Frank and I embrace like old, close friends unaware of the quarter of a century that separates us.

Inside, we find Deidra Baxley and Sandy Pickler at a booth beneath a hanging blue light.

Tonight the Landmark is quiet and mostly empty, its mirrored surfaces reflecting other objects instead of patrons, its glass and metal surfaces having very little conversation reverberate off of them.

"Sandy, John," Deidra says. "John, Sandy."

"Nice to meet you," I say and shake her hand. "Deidra, Sandy, Frank," I add. "Frank, Deidra and Sandy."

"It's been a while since I've enjoyed a late supper with ladies so lovely," Frank says. "Order what you want 'cause tonight dinner is on me."

I blink back tears as I remember the times when I was a seriously broke college student that Frank not only took me to eat, but slipped a twenty or fifty or hundred in my pocket.

As I had hoped, Frank and the two lovely but broken ladies become fast friends and before long Frank is volunteering to help with security and some light maintenance at Myra House.

"I still have friends on the force," Frank says, "so I can also help deal with anybody who's harassing or threatening y'all too."

"Keep it up," Deidra says, "and I just might ask you to marry me."

He smiles and maybe even blushes a bit, but acts as though she's joking, which I'm pretty sure she is, but even if she isn't, Frank's feelings on the matter are unalterable. He's had his one great true love and will only have it again if there's a life after this one.

Beneath the table, I pull out my phone and text Susan. *I'm at Landmark Diner. Remembering your birthdays here and so many of the great times we shared. Just wanted to say I'm grateful for what we had and the amazing daughter we produced.*

After we've all eaten more than we should have, and Sandy is working her way through the largest slice of coconut cake in the metro area, she says, "I want to live again."

"You will," Deidra says. "You're on your way. Think about how far you've come."

"But I'm so ... weak and needy. If I didn't have you to prop me up. I'm like Myra House in that way—fall apart if you're not around. You can't go away without us falling to pieces. You're gone for a few days and we—"

"Survived just fine," Deidra says.

"Wouldn't say just fine."

"Well, you did."

"Not everyone did. Two of the women actually left. Went back to their batterers."

"You're stronger than you think you are," Deidra says. "You'll only need our support for a little while and then it'll be you supporting others. Just wait. You'll see."

My phone vibrates and I pull it back out of my pocket. It's Susan texting back. *Wouldn't change a thing. Except maybe it ending. But no regrets. Thanks for thinking of me and appreciating us. Eat a big piece of cake for me.*

"That's an awful lot of pressure on you," Frank says to Deidra.

Deidra smiles. "Nice to be needed."

"We're like the needy children she never had," Sandy says.

"Maybe I can help with some of that pressure," Frank says. "And I know some kickass female cops who would love to volunteer—mentor, help in any way they can, teach self-defense classes."

"Self-defense would be good," Sandy says, "but the most

important thing is us learning what good, decent men are and how to be attracted to them."

"I think Special Agent Frank here will help with that," Deidra says, a certain twinkle in her eyes. "Think havin' him around will help with that just fine."

"He's truly one of the best men I've ever known," I say. "Can't think of a better man for the job."

37

M ariah's funeral service is as heartbreaking as any I've ever attended.

It's inside the small chapel of Williams Family Funeral Home in Decatur.

I'm sitting toward the back on a pew with Frank Morgan, Deidra Baxley and her parents, Pick and Rhonda Baxley.

The small sanctuary is filled with invited family and friends whose names are on a strictly-enforced list. Several reporters, armchair detectives, and morbidly curious crashers who attempted to sneak in were turned away by Merrill and other security guards working the door because their names weren't on the list.

Merrill is one among many bodyguards and security guarding all the entrances and escorting the family in and out.

Outside, there are more media vans set up than the parking lot and surrounding area can accommodate. We all entered the building to the sounds of cameras clicking, reporters both broad-casting and yelling questions at us.

Trace, did you kill your daughter?

How did Mariah die?

Is it true she was found naked tied up in the bathtub?

Was duct tape found in her esophagus?

Is Mariah the black JonBenét?

Investigator Jordan, are you here to arrest Trace Evidence for the murder of his daughter?

Was this a gangland style hit? Trace, was this a message? Is your past catching up with you?

What about the rumors that you're gay? Is Ashley just your beard? Was this the work of one of your gay lovers?

Is it true Mariah isn't really dead? Did you fake her death for the publicity?

Does rap music promote violence? Did your music and lifestyle lead to your daughter's death?

After an awkward greeting from a shaky elderly minister who has some connection to the family through Trace's grandmother I believe, and the reading of the obituary, two large women in dresses several sizes too small sing a soulful, a cappella version of Amazing Grace.

At the conclusion of the song, a large screen descends from the ceiling at the center of the platform and a professionally produced montage video that includes both pictures and home movie footage is projected onto the screen from a projector mounted on the ceiling.

It's difficult to watch, impossible not to. And the disconnect between watching this energetic, enthusiastic little full-of-life performer and knowing her lifeless body is inside the too-small coffin below it causes an existential dissonance like few I've ever experienced.

On the other side of Frank, the stoic Baxley family shed silent tears, their devastation no less real for the quiet nature of their dignified mourning. And seeing the kind of people they are and how they carry and conduct themselves convince me all the more that Trace hasn't been truthful with us.

Others throughout the congregation cry loudly, sobbing and saying *Je-sus* often.

The eulogy is far better than I expected it to be, and includes the reading of letters from Mariah's classmates who genuinely seem to adore her. The speaker, Mariah's school teacher, Miss Amy, captures the kind, funny, precocious child, who we learn was an accomplished prankster and a bit of a tomboy, better than anyone else could.

When Trace, Ashley, and Brett rise, each with a single white rose in their hand, and walk toward the small coffin, I get my first real look at them since the service began. Ashley is hidden beneath an enormous black hat and veil, Brett, who doesn't look like himself without a handheld video game device in his hand, is holding his mother's hand and appearing disaffected, but Trace, whose knees buckle as he places the rose on the coffin, is clearly visible, the dark shades he wears unable to hide the obvious pain and genuine anguish etched on the brittle, too-tight skin of his face.

As he falls, he grabs Mariah's tiny coffin for support.

I can't imagine the stand the coffin is on is strong or stable enough to support him, but it does, and Trace remains upright.

Though slow to respond, Ashley eventually reaches over and offers support.

When they arrive back at their seats on the front row, Brett still has his rose. Ashley leans down, whispers something to him, and he takes a few steps forward and tosses the rose at the coffin.

The rose hits the side of the small coffin and bounces off, landing on the floor, as Brett returns to his seat.

In a sudden burst of anger, Trace steps over, grabs Brett by the arm, and snatches him up off the pew and drags him over to the rose. Shoving him down toward the rose without letting go of his grip on his arm, he yells *Pick it up*, then, after Brett has the rose in his hand, drags him to the coffin and waits while he carefully places it on top with the two others.

When Trace releases Brett, he runs over to his mother, who wraps him up in her arms and comforts him.

Trace returns to his spot on the pew and for the rest of day he and Ashley don't touch or speak.

38

Merrill reacts first.

Frank and I shortly after him.

Then the other bodyguard Trace employs.

We have just reached the parking lot out in front of the funeral home, witnessed Mariah's coffin being loaded by the pallbearers into the glass horse-drawn carriage that will transport her to the nearby cemetery.

As soon as the door of the carriage is closed, the reporters begin to yell their questions.

How was the service? Trace? Trace? What do you have to say to those who say you should be in jail instead of out here at your victim's funeral? Where will Mariah be buried? Will she be laid to rest beside her mother? Trace? Did you kill her mother too?

Everyone is rushing to their vehicles to avoid the assault of the reporters and their cameras that make what are normal reactions to the vile questions they're asking look irreverent or suspicious or worse.

Thankfully most everyone is in or near, and therefore shielded by, their vehicle when it happens.

I'm scanning the area as Deidra is helping her parents look for their car when it happens.

I see Merrill reach for his gun and move toward the street.

I follow his gaze as I reach beneath my suit coat and withdraw my weapon and begin to yell for everyone to get down and take cover.

Frank does the same.

A big black SUV with illegally dark tinted windows cruises by out on the small side street that fronts the funeral home, its back passenger side window rolling down, the barrel of a rifle being brought up and out.

I shove Deidra and her parents and few others around me down and continue to yell.

Screaming.

Running.

Falling.

Ducking.

Jumping in vehicles. Ducking behind them.

The moment the first round is fired, Merrill fires back.

Panic.

Pandemonium.

The pool of reporters is caught in the crossfire. Some turn their attention and cameras toward the SUV. Others drop to the ground. Still others knock over tripods and lights and mic stands in attempt to get to the nearest place of cover.

Merrill is running toward the SUV, firing as it does.

The shooter in the SUV fires the rifle a few times, picking and choosing his targets carefully. Most of his rounds go into the limo Trace and his family hide behind.

Several of Merrill's rounds hit the SUV.

As the back window of the vehicle rises, the SUV speeds away.

All of us strain to see the plate as it does, but there isn't one.

Less than a minute after it all began, it's over.

We walk around surveying the damage as the reporters begin broadcasting live.

Deidra's dad has a gunshot wound to his left hand and Trace has fragments of asphalt and shards of glass from rounds ricocheting around him in his face.

All other wounds appear superficial and self-inflicted.

39

"See?" Deidra says. "You thought I was being paranoid."

I shake my head. "No. I didn't."

She and her mother are standing at the back of an ambulance where EMTs are working on her father's injury.

"I told you he'd try something, didn't I?"

"He got hit too," I say, turning toward another ambulance across the way where EMTs are picking glass and bits of rock out of Trace's face.

"Which was either an accident or a brilliant cover," she says.

Against the advice of the EMTs, both Pick and Trace are refusing to go to the hospital, opting instead for some minor triage so they can attend the graveside.

Pick had said, "It's just a scratch. I'm fine. Lot of blood, but it's just the tip of my little finger."

When Deidra had turned to her mom and said, "Tell him he has to go to the hospital," Rhonda had shaken her head.

"I can't get him to do anything, you know that," Rhonda said. "Besides, I understand what he's saying. We haven't seen our granddaughter since she was a baby and we're going to miss part of her funeral . . . I don't think so."

Trace had said, "Nigga with a gun not gonna run me off from laying my little girl to rest. Promise you that. They gonna have to kill me to keep me from burying my baby."

While they're getting treated, Merrill, Frank, and I step away from everyone to talk.

"Nice work out there," Frank says to Merrill.

"You too."

"We were just following your lead."

I nod.

"Just hope I didn't just help save the life of a child killer."

"There were a lot of lives at stake," I say. "Not just his."

Dekalb Sheriff's department is looking for the vehicle," Frank says. "Sure it's stolen and will be empty by the time they find it, but . . . could lead us to the shooter."

"Not your typical drive-by, was it?" Merrill says. "Shooter fired very few rounds and at specific places."

I nod.

"Usually see an automatic or semi-auto and the shooter sprays the crowd," Frank says.

"More a hit than a drive-by," I say. "Or supposed to look like it anyway. Not sure exactly what that was."

"I'm gonna find out," Frank says. "Got some friends at the bureau . . . call in some favors."

"Need to look at Rondarious Swaggart," I say. "Rapper that goes by the name Little Swag. He's made threats against Trace. I've tried to see him since I've been in town, but haven't been able to."

"Leave it with me," Frank says. "I'll track down Little Swag."

"Think we have to look at him for Mariah's murder too," I say.

"Consider it done."

Frank and I walk back toward Pick's ambulance as Merrill makes his way over to Trace's.

"Help me out," Pick says to me and Frank. "I want to be on my feet before he is."

We do.

"Kill my daughter and granddaughter and try to kill me at her funeral," he says, looking over in Trace's direction. "Well, I don't kill so easy."

"*Dad*," Deidra says, her voice scolding though she is smiling.

"He's right," Rhonda says. "He took our daughter and our granddaughter from us. We're burying her today, but Mariah's been dead to us since he killed Myra. That . . . animal saw to that. We missed her entire life and then he's gonna try to shoot us when we dare to come to her funeral. Screw that. Screw him."

Deidra suppresses a smile at her mom's use of *screw*.

"Don't laugh at me, Deidra," she says. "Do I have to use stronger language for you not to laugh at me?"

"I wasn't laughing at you, Mom. Hearing you talk like that made me happy. That's all. I say *screw him* too."

40

I wake up the next morning next to Anna.

I drove all night to be able to. And to say it was worth it would be the understatement of the century.

The moment my eyes blink open, she slides closer, cuddling with me.

"Morning," I whisper.

"Morning. I've been wanting to touch you so badly it's been driving me crazy, but I didn't want to wake you."

"Don't ever not wake me," I say.

I turn to look at the girls.

They're not in their beds in here like they were when I slipped in here this morning.

"Where are—"

"Your dad and Verna took them to the park."

"What time is it?"

"Nine."

"*Nine?*"

I reach over and lift my phone from the nightstand. I have several texts and missed calls—three from Reggie.

"You got in so late I wanted to let you sleep," she says.

"Thank you," I say, returning the phone to the nightstand.

"And with the girls away I thought we might take advantage of some uninterrupted alone time."

"I was thinking the same thing," I say. "Why I didn't call Reggie back."

"I wanted to give everyone a chance to share what they've got and go over the evidence that's coming in," Reggie says.

It's early afternoon. Arnie, Keisha, Jessica, and I are in Reggie's office.

"Oh, and to welcome Sleeping Beauty back from Atlanta," she adds, smiling at me. "He's the reason we postponed the meeting from this morning."

"Glad to have you back in one piece," Arnie says. "We heard about the drive-by."

"Heard, hell," Keisha says. "Watched that shit on YouTube."

"You, Merrill, and that GBI agent prevented a massacre," Arnie adds. "Good work."

I'm not sure we did, but I thank him.

"I'm'a need you to introduce me to that Merrill man," Keisha says.

We all laugh.

"Any updates on that so far?" Reggie says.

I shake my head. "GBI and Dekalb County Sheriff are looking into it, but nothing so far."

"Shame the shooter didn't at least clip a few of those reporters," Keisha says.

"From what they're reporting," Arnie says, "they know a lot more about our case than we do."

"Shit they're sayin' is vile," Keisha says. "All of 'em too. It's like there's only one kind of journalism anymore—tabloid."

"Can't let verifiable truth get in the way of entertainment," I say.

"They're makin' it near 'bout impossible for us to make a case," Keisha says. "And forget finding a jury who hasn't been tainted."

"Well, we're gonna build a case and we're going to take the killer to trial," Reggie says, "so let's get to it. Who wants to start?"

"I will," Jessica says.

"Okay."

"Only prints in the safe room are Roger Garrett's and Justin Harris's," she says. "And there's no other physical evidence in it—no blood or . . . nothing to indicate the killer was in there before or after Mariah's murder."

"Everywhere we turn, every new piece of evidence we find or don't find," Keisha says, "makes it look like the killer was someone staying in the house that night."

Reggie nods. "I agree."

"I think I may have something," Arnie says, "and if I'm right about it, it could be evidence of an intruder or not—could go either way."

"What's that?" Reggie asks.

"Remember the little metal pieces found on the floor in Mariah's bedroom?"

"Yeah," Reggie says.

"They're still at the lab," Jessica says.

"Here's a picture of them," he says, and passes around an evidence photo of the small flat piece of metal with the small cylindrical piece beside it.

"Now look at this," he says, and passes another photo showing two similar pieces.

"They're the same, right?"

Reggie Nods.

Jessica says, "Look the same to me."

"That flat piece is a blast door," Arnie says. "The little round thing is part of a probe. They're from a taser."

"Great work, Arnie," I say. "Really nice. That's exactly what it is."

"Nice job, partner," Keisha says.

"Yes," Reggie says. "Very nice. So . . . hopefully we'll get prints or DNA or something from it, but . . . in the meantime the use of a taser argues for an intruder, right?"

"You'd think anyone in the house—except maybe Irvin and Brett could just tell Mariah what to do and she'd do it," Keisha says. "Trace, Ashley, and Nadine—I mean, she'd do what they told her to, wouldn't she?"

"That's what I was thinkin'," Arnie says.

"So maybe there was an intruder," Reggie says. "But with no break-in . . ."

"We're back to someone with a key or someone hiding in the house after the party," Keisha says.

"John?" Reggie says. "What's that look? What're you thinking?"

"Two things," I say. "That it doesn't necessarily point to an intruder or Brett or Irvin—though it might. It could just be part of the killer's sick fantasy or some form of punishment, a desire to control or inflict pain prior to death."

"True," Keisha says, "so it could be Trace playing some sick sexual game or Ashley being punitive in some sick way."

"But," I say, "and this is by far the more important point. There's absolutely no evidence in Mariah's autopsy that a taser was used on her."

41

"Saw you on YouTube," Randa Raffield says.

I'm driving home for the day, bone-weary and mentally exhausted, the slash pines lining the rural highway seen through my raindrop-dotted windshield all running together.

It has been a while since she's called—so long, in fact, that when I saw the call was from an unknown number I didn't even consider it might be her. Of course that could have something to do with the weariness as well.

"You did just fine," she adds, "but Merrill was particularly impressive."

"Yes he was."

"Makes you wonder why he didn't do a better job of protecting Daniel, doesn't it? Was he just having an off night or am I just that good?"

"He'd welcome a rematch anytime," I say.

"Speaking of Daniel . . . How's our boy doing? He missing mama yet? Give him my love, would you?"

I don't respond.

The drizzling rain intensifies a bit and I turn my wipers up a notch.

"Well anyway," she says, "I was just calling to ask for your autograph now that you're all internet famous and shit. And to make sure we're square."

"*Square?*"

"Since I returned ol' Dan. Wanted to make sure you were keeping your end of the bargain and not still looking for me."

"We're nothing like square," I say. "And we've never had a bargain, but you don't even keep the ones you make without my agreement. But I'll be honest with you . . . I'm not actively looking for you right now."

"Got your hands full, do you?"

"Little bit, yeah."

"Well, it's for the best," she says. "There's no extradition here. It's why I'm here. And I'd hate to see you throw a lot of effort after futility."

"That's sweet of you, thanks."

"I like you, John," she says. "Always have. That's why I want you to leave me alone. Don't want to have to tussle with you or wind up hurting someone you love. And let's face it, you love a lot of people. You're obviously not Buddhist, are you? By my calculations you've got more than your share of woes."

I smile, appreciating her allusion to statement attributed to the Buddha that *He who loves 50 people has 50 woes. He who loves no one has no woes.*

"Makes you very vulnerable," she says.

"In one sense, sure. But in another just the opposite."

"Maybe."

"You sayin' you have no woes?" I ask. "That'd be a very sad way to live."

"I'm not a—Do you think I'm a sociopath, John? Do you? I'm not. I feel. I love. I have a conscience. And just because it's not calibrated the same as yours doesn't make it bad."

"Never said anything like that. Never would. I'm certainly not saying my calibration is any better than anyone else's. You seem a little touchy about it, though. Might be something to look into."

"I might just do that," she says, "while I'm sipping on Sex on the Beaches and soaking in the sun, I'll give it some thought. Oh, and I'll be thinking about your Black JonBenét case too. That's what those fucks are callin' it, you know. Anyway, if you need help with it just let me know."

42

"The prints are the nightmare we thought they'd be," Jessica says. "But there doesn't seem to be any real big surprises. Not really."

It's later that night and she's calling because Reggie told her to the moment she had gone over the results. So instead of waiting until the next morning and telling us all at the same time in the office, she is calling all four of us individually and going over it with us.

"Lay it on me," I say.

"The nightmare part is just how very many prints there are," she says. "Hundreds. Because of the party, I guess. We've identified some of those—the ones of family and friends who we printed and got writing samples from—but there are hundreds more that we don't have matches for. A defense team would have a field day with it. We've got the guest list, but I haven't heard if we're going to try to print everyone on it or not. That's a Reggie call, but . . . can't imagine it will do much good. No way we can find them all. And what about the crashers? We don't even know who they are."

I think about what she's saying and what we might do

about it.

"And evidently some guests toured the house while at the party," she says. "Their prints aren't just downstairs. They're on all three levels—Ashley's mother and brother, Arlene and Hank, Jr., but they're not in her bedroom, just the hallway, doorjambs, staircase, bathrooms, things like that."

"Okay," I say, "we'll get to the broader house, but let's start with Nicole's room."

"*Nicole?*"

"Sorry," I say. "Mariah's."

"Who's Nicole?"

"Sorry about that," I say. "A victim in another case. Certain things about Mariah remind me of her. Been thinking about her and . . . Let's zoom in on Mariah's room first, then pull back and look at the rest of the house."

"Sure," she says. "Like I said, no huge surprises. Of course Mariah's are all over, as are Brett's."

"There are a lot of Brett's?" I ask.

"Nearly as many as Mariah's," she says. "There are less but still a good bit of Trace's, Ashley's—and probably more of Nadine's than the two of theirs put together. The aunt's are on the picture frame and earrings like she told you."

While I was in Atlanta I got fingerprints and handwriting samples from Nadine, Deidra, Pick, Rhonda, and a couple of Trace's friends and bodyguards who were at the party on the third.

"Andy Finch's," she continues, "Ronnie Wyric's, and Arnie's are also in the room—mostly on the doorjamb."

"Can't believe they didn't wear gloves," I say. "But I didn't think Andy went in—oh, I guess when he first searched the house. Okay."

"There's a lot of one other as-yet-unidentified set of prints," she says. "And they're pretty much all over the place."

"From a smaller hand?" I ask.

"Yeah."

"I figure that's from the little boy from next door who played with them," I say. "Caden Stevens. I'll get his prints when I interview him."

"Great. I'll get them processed and compared when you do."

"How about Irvin?" I ask.

"One partial."

"So he was in there at some point."

"Yep. Now, the entire house was cleaned before the family arrived—and we have several of the maid's prints everywhere, including Mariah's room and bathroom—so . . . I was surprised to see some of both the owner and rental agent in her room."

"They found both Roger Garrett's and Justin Harris's prints in Mariah's bedroom?"

"Yep."

"Thought you said there weren't any big surprises?"

"Well, it's not like we found the Zodiac's or OJ's."

"Where were they?"

"Justin's are sort of all over the place—it's that way in the rest of the house too—on and round both the bedroom and the bathroom doors, on the bed, one the—"

"All the beds or just Mariah's?"

"Just Mariah's. On the wall near her bed and the windowsill on the left."

"Where were Garrett's?" I ask.

"Partial palm print on the bedside table," she says.

"Was it in a place that the maid might miss when she cleans?"

"No, not really. It was right there on the top front like he leaned on it. They way you'd expect if he were maybe leaning down over the bed. And there's another thing that makes it very suspicious—there's not a single other print of his in the entire house—not even the safe room."

"Sometime," I say, "we're gonna have to talk about your definition of *big surprises*."

43

That night I dream of JonBenét.

I'm a detective assigned to her case.

I'm in conflict with my colleagues over what I perceive as their too-narrow focus and the influence they're letting the media have on the investigation.

Walking through the house. JonBenét beside me. Alive. Helping me solve her murder. She is who she was before she was killed and doesn't know who killed her any more than I do.

Unlike the media portrayal of her, she is and acts like a typical kid. Active. Energetic. Entertaining.

Suddenly she is with me in Roger Garrett's mansion on Cape San Blas.

She's motioning for me to bend down to tell me a secret.

I know who killed Mariah, she whispers.

Who?

The bad, bad man.

With no warning or transition, I am back in the Ramsey home in Boulder, but this time Mariah is leading me through the house.

Do you know who killed JonBenét? I ask.

The bad, bad man, she says. *He killed me too.*

Not the same man, I say. *You don't mean that.*

No, not the same. I don't mean that.

We climb a spiral staircase.

John, why do the innocent suffer? Why is there so much pain in this world?

I shake my head. *I don't know. I'm so sorry. I wish I did. I wish I could take it back, make it stop, undo what has been done, but I can't. And I can't explain it. Please forgive me. I'm sorry I can't.*

I feel terrible regret and guilt at not being able to give her the answer she seeks. I feel as though I should be able to and it bothers me more than I can say that I can't.

Do you think it'll do any good to catch who killed me?

I do, I say. *Will it not? Am I wrong? I believe it will help or I wouldn't be doing it.*

Won't help me, she says.

No, It won't help you. Do you not want me to?

I wanted to live, she says, wistfully. *To love a boy. To get my ears pierced. To learn to drive. To make a record of my own one day. Just to live.*

Tears start streaming down my cheeks.

Anna and I are at dinner. We're talking about adopting Mariah as a way of saving her, removing her from the environment and situation that led to her death.

And then—

Then I'm awake and my cheeks are damp and my heart hurts and I feel as if I'm in a shroud of deep darkness and sadness I can't slough off.

44

"I miss you man," I say. "How much longer you gonna be up there?"

It's the next morning and I'm talking to Merrill by phone on my drive out to the Cape to meet Justin Harris and Roger Garrett.

"Was supposed to already be back," he says, "but after the shooting at the funeral home, he asked me to stay on a couple'a extra days. Said I would, but . . . not sure how long any this gonna last. They's all kinds of trouble in paradise."

"Oh yeah?"

"Miss Nadine quit," he says. "Already gone."

"She told me she was done, that she had only been there for Mariah."

"Yeah. I think it hit her harder than anyone."

"Told me it was like losing her own daughter," I say.

The day is gray and overcast, the morning sun hidden by clouds. The ground is still wet and another storm is gathering in the distance.

"Can't imagine Trace and Ashley are gonna be together much longer," he says. "Be surprised if she hasn't moved out by the end of the week."

"Does it seem mutual?" I ask. "Or more one than the other?"

"Hard to tell . . . Times I think it's more him wanting her gone. Others seems like what she wants—more for Brett than herself maybe. Not sure."

"Figured after the way Trace snatched Brett around at the funeral . . ."

"Yeah, it's that . . . but not just *that*. From what I gather, they weren't really havin' problems before Mariah's murder."

Makes me wonder if one suspects the other—or maybe more than suspects. Knows.

"And it's not just losing Mariah," he says. "Which is the main thing. But . . . looks like Trace is losing everything. Tours and sponsorships and albums and TV appearances are being canceled. Says nobody returning his calls. Think he's feelin' pretty damn isolated. And the media's still houndin' hell out of him. Always at the house. Everywhere he goes. And the shit they sayin' about him and her and even Mariah is . . . It's fucked up. All that pressure makin' things 'round here ready to explode or implode or somethin'."

"Have there been any other threats or assaults or anything?"

"No."

"Probably won't be after they see your YouTube video."

"Not 'less they suicidal," he says with a laugh.

"Randa was impressed by it," I say.

"She call back, tell her to come see me, I'll give her a private demonstration."

"Already told her you said *anytime*."

"Hope like hell she takes me up on the offer," he says.

"Me too."

"Looks like they comin' downstairs," he says. "Better go so I can guard them while they eat their cornflakes."

"I appreciate the information," I say.

"I ain't sayin' one or both of 'em did it 'cause I don't have a clue who did," he says, "but I am sayin' 'round 'bout now be a good time for those follow-up interviews."

With about ten minutes left of my drive, I call Frank Morgan.

"I could kiss you, son," he says.

"Why's that?"

"Getting me this gig," he says, "Haven't felt this useful in a while. Quite a while. And the cause . . . the cause is so damn righteous. I mean . . . these poor women. The work they do here is . . . extraordinary. Feels so good to help them out. And I'm not just doing security. Deidra says it's good for the women to be around a decent and gentle man. I'm actually helpin' with their recovery and reprograming."

"That's great," I say. "So good. You're the perfect man for the job."

"Spent so much of my career chasing down the lowlifes after they had killed or raped or assaulted someone. So different to help prevent them from doing that instead of tryin' to catch them afterwards."

"Speaking of chasin' down bad guys," I say, "anything happening on the shooter?"

"Found the vehicle," he says. "It was abandoned and torched. Had been stolen. Even still . . . I hear there're some good leads. Should know something soon."

"Good."

"Not sayin' it's him, but . . . guess who's nowhere to be found?"

"Little Swag?"

"How can you say that without laughing?" he says.

"It's not easy."

45

I arrive at Roger Garrett's Stars Haven mansion to discover his attorney is with him.

"My client is not responsible nor can be held liable for what another person does in one of his rental properties," Hugh Browning III says.

"Nobody's saying he is or can be," I say.

"Then why ask to see him?" he asks.

Justin Harris acts nervous and looks as if he's uncomfortable with conflict.

"Just wanted to ask him about the house and where he was on the night of the Fourth."

We're standing in the living room on the main floor. Around us the house is in disarray, as if a crime scene unit has tromped though it. Fingerprint dust around doors, on walls, and other hard surfaces. Evidence markers strewn about. Crime scene tape across the exterior doors, its ragged ends flapping in the Gulf breeze.

"Why? Surely, you're not suggesting he's even a suspect. We already submitted fingerprints and handwriting samples . . . this is just too—"

"You know how this works," I say. "We have to eliminate everyone we can so we can narrow our focus onto—"

"I know that's what y'all always say," he says. "But . . . in my experience I find that y'all spread a lot of suspicion about but rarely publicly clear anyone."

"An arrest is the best way to clear everyone else," I say. "That's what we're working toward. It's why I'm here. Why I'm tryin' to eliminate any and every one I can."

"I'll talk to him, Hugh," Roger Garrett says. "Quit bein' such a little bitch about it." He looks at me. "What is it you want to know?"

"Before today, when's the last time you were in the house?"

He looks up and appears to think about it. "Not sure. Been a while, though. Only came today to say goodbye to the place."

"You're selling it?"

He nods. "Got some true crime nut makin' me an offer I can't refuse. But he insists that nobody rents it or uses it and that we don't clean anything. Wants all the fingerprint dust left where it is, the carpet cut up, the evidence tape and markers."

"Who is it?"

He shakes his head. "He insists on anonymity for the deal to go through, so . . . It'll be public record as soon as the deed is recorded."

I wonder if it's the killer trying to destroy evidence. Of our actual suspects, only Trace could afford it.

"When is closing?" I ask.

"I'm sorry," he says, "but I don't want to say exactly. I'm not tryin' to be difficult or uncooperative, but I don't want y'all setting up some sort of sting at the title agency or my real estate attorney's office."

"Will you at least tell me if it's soon?" I say. "Is he in a hurry?"

"He's already told you, detective," Browning says. "He doesn't want to—"

"It's soon," Garrett says. "And he does seem in a mighty big hurry, which is just fine with me. I used to love this place, but no more. It's . . . forever spoiled for me."

"Did you remember when the last time you'd been in was?"

"Have to be back in the spring sometime, I'd say. Can't be more specific than that."

"Do you have the maid clean your safe room?" I ask.

Garrett whips his head around and stares at Justin, who has been so quiet I'd almost forgotten he was there.

"You're worse than a damn woman, Justin," he says. "Can't keep a secret for shit."

"Sorry, Mr. Garrett. I thought they already knew about it. But I mean . . . it's a . . . murder investigation."

"Good thing I've got nothin' to hide," he says. "Not even my goddamn top secret hidden room."

He looks back at me.

"No," he says. "I do not. I would've said none of them even knew about its existence, but Mr. Can't Keep A Secret over here probably told them too."

"Who cleans it?" I ask. "How often?"

"To my knowledge no one," he says. "I'm the only one who uses it—or so I thought." He turns back toward Justin. "You been going in my room? Take your girlfriend or wife or whatever? Throw parties down there."

"No, Sir. Never. Absolutely not. No, sir."

"Bad enough you rented my big blue masterpiece to some low rent jigaboo child killers," he says. "Now you tell everyone about my room."

He looks back at me. "It's supposed to be a secret. That's the point. Not really worth havin' otherwise. It probably needs cleanin' 'cause I've never cleaned it, but I'm not much of a maid. What's with all the questions about the last time I've been in the house or safe room and if I clean it?"

"Because I'm wondering why your prints are inside the victim's bedroom and why they're *not* in your safe room."

"Okay," Browning says. "That's it. This little discussion is over. Not another word, Roger. You have any other questions for my client, submit them to me in writing, understand?"

Garrett starts to say something, but Browning stops him.

"I'm serious as fuck, Roger," he says. "Not another goddamn word."

"That went well," Justin says.

Garrett and Browning are gone. Justin and I are alone in the huge house.

"You probably just cost me my business," he adds.

"How?"

"I'm about to go under as it is," he says. "Without him as a client, I'm done. Did you have to mention the hidden room?"

I nod. "But I didn't know I wasn't supposed to," I say. "I'm sorry. Didn't intentionally try to jam you up."

He frowns and nods.

"Business really that bad?" I ask. "Thought things were booming out here."

"My situation is dire, but . . . I'm sure not everybody's is."

"Sorry to hear that."

"Speaking of . . . I need to get back to the office. Try to figure out a way to win Mr. Garrett back."

"You're not handling the sale of this house?"

He shakes his head. "Didn't even know about it until he just mentioned it. God, if I was . . ."

"What would it take you to get flush?" I ask.

"Not much. Not compared to what my business is worth—or what these homes out here sell for. A twelfth of what this house alone is worth would have me back in the black."

"What's he getting for it?" I ask.

He shrugs. "Not sure. Sounds like his buyer is paying a

premium, but I'd say the market value is about three mil. I really do need to go."

"Okay," I say, "I'll make this quick. When you were together, was Ashley into bondage? Submission? Being tied up?"

After giving me a look that conveys both confusion and disgust, he shakes his head. "*No.* To be honest . . . Well, anyway. No, she wasn't."

"*To be honest* what?" I ask.

"Nothing. I don't know why I even—You just proved you can't keep a secret."

"I didn't know it was a secret."

"It's a *secret* room for fuck sake."

"You know what I mean. What were you going to say?"

"Just that . . . Ashley was kind of pedestrian in bed. Kind of boring. And I beg of you not to ever tell her I said anything like that. I wouldn't hurt her feelings for anything."

"I won't. You have my word."

"Can I go now?"

"How well is a house like this cleaned before a new guest arrives?"

"Immaculately. Extremely. Spotlessly. You don't pay what you do for a place like this and it not be pristine in every way. Why?"

"Just trying to account for the evidence we found," I say. "Particularly prints."

"Do you realize how many people were here during the party?" he says. "We were all over the place. Touching everything."

"I'm sure that's it," I say, as if I actually am.

46

"Handwriting results are back," Reggie says.

We are back in her office—me, Arnie, Keisha, and Jessica—at the end of the day to share information and coordinate our efforts.

Though it's hours before sunset, the day is dark and thunder can be heard in the distance.

"On both notes," she adds. "First, the runaway note alleged to have been written by Mariah . . . actually was. Her handwriting is a match. She did write that note."

She pauses to let that sink in. And we do.

"As far as the ransom note . . ." she says eventually, "everyone we've gotten samples from can be excluded but four people. Anybody want to guess who they are?"

Nobody does.

"I'm disappointed," she says. "What if I give y'all a clue? Two of the people are from inside the house and two are from out."

Nobody says anything.

"No fun at all," she says. "Okay. The two inside . . . are . . . Trace and Irvin."

She pauses again to let it sink in. And again we do.

Keisha and Arnie nod like what's said is what they had expected.

"And outside?" Keisha asks.

"Hank Howard," she says, "and Justin Harris."

"Both of whom have a connection to Ashley," Keisha says. "Brother and ex-husband."

"This doesn't necessarily mean one of them wrote it," Jessica says. "Just that they can't be eliminated."

"Everyone else has been eliminated," Reggie says. "That's good to know . . . 'Cause my money was on Ashley. That's why we follow the evidence and not our guts."

"So what's our next step?" Keisha says.

"Additional handwriting samples," Jessica says.

"Right," Reggie says. "We've got very specific lists of words and sentences we want them to write for us—with both their left and right hands. But . . . we're also going to try to find random samples of their writing on other things—checks, letters, lists. Unguarded. Unrehearsed. Real and raw as we can find. Means sifting through their garbage. Whatever it takes."

"We have Trace's song journal," I say. "Should be plenty."

"Be a good place to start," she says. "Okay, let's figure out who's doing what. We've got two in the area, two in Atlanta. Do we want to let the Dekalb County sheriff's do it or take care of it ourselves?"

"I think we need to," Keisha says. "I don't mind driving to Atlanta." She turns to Arnie. "You up for a little road trip, partner?"

He nods.

"Okay," Reggie says, and looks over at me.

"I'll take Howard and Harris," I say.

Jessica says, "Is not being able to eliminate these men based on their handwriting enough to get a search warrant? No tellin' what we might find if we could take a look through their things."

"Probably not," Reggie says. "We'll need to narrow it down some more. But even if we get a match after this next round . . . handwriting analysis isn't an exact science. Even if we could convince a judge to give us a warrant it could probably be easily appealed, which means anything we found would be fruits of a poisonous tree. We'd lose it all. Can't afford that. The handwriting evidence will help strengthen a case made against someone we get other evidence on."

"Just thought the killer might have some evidence we could use or maybe he kept a memento."

"Like her iPod," I say.

"Yeah," Jessica says.

"It's truly amazing," Reggie says, "even knowing they should destroy any and all evidence, how many killers don't. Maybe we'll get lucky. We're getting close folks. I want to get Trace and Ashley and Irvin and Nadine back down here for questioning soon, but I want our case built by then. We'll have DNA results in a little while. Let's keep at it. Work fast but carefully."

"I've got an idea I'd like for us to try," Arnie says.

"What's that?"

"Our main two suspects are together a lot," he says. "Trace and Irvin. The media is still hounding them relentlessly. From what I hear Trace is slowly losing everything—including Ashley. Probably never be under more stress than he is right now."

"Yeah?"

"And Mariah's birthday is coming up soon. I think we should coordinate with the GBI to get Trace's house mic'd up. His car and Mariah's headstone too. No tellin' what's all being said right now. Could lead to the information we need—maybe even a confession. I could picture Trace and Ashley saying incriminating things in an argument or Trace going to Mariah's grave on her birthday and breaking down and apologizing to her for what he did."

Something similar was done in the JonBenét Ramsey case. It didn't yield anything useful, but that doesn't mean this wouldn't.

"That's a great idea," she says. "Not sure I can pull it off, but it's worth a try. That really could work if we could actually do it. I'll see what I can do. Good thinkin' Arnie."

47

On my way to get additional handwriting samples from Hank Howard, I call Justin Harris to schedule a time to meet with him to do the same thing.

"I don't think so, John," he says. "I . . . just . . . I've lost confidence in the investigation, in your department . . . and . . . I've cooperated . . . I've been so cooperative, but . . . I don't know, the things I'm hearing being reported . . . I just think y'all are getting desperate to pin it on somebody and I don't want that to be me. I've hired Mr. Browning and he said—"

"You and Roger Garrett have the same attorney?" I ask.

"We do."

I know Justin can't afford Hugh Browning, so either Garrett is paying for it for some reason or Browning is providing his services pro bono. Either way it's more than a little suspicious.

"Is Roger Garrett still your client?" I ask.

"What does that have to do with—"

"Earlier you accused me of costing you his business and making yours go under."

"He's still a client, but that has nothing to do with—well, anything really."

"Is he paying for Hugh Browning for you?"

"That's not—that has nothing to do with who murdered Mariah."

"Why would he pay for your attorney?" I ask. "Why would he want it to be the same as his? Do you have something on him? Is that how you're keeping him as a client?"

"Anyway, good luck with the case," he says. "I hope you get the guy. I really do. But don't contact me again. If you need anything in the future, call my attorney."

He hangs up without saying *goodbye* and I call Reggie.

"Justin is refusing to give any more handwriting samples or to cooperate in any way," I say.

"Oh, really?"

"And he's lawyered up."

"Interesting."

"Even more so when you hear who his attorney is."

"Who's that?"

"Hugh Browning."

"Thought he only worked for Roger Garrett?"

"My guess is that's who's picking up the tab."

"Extremely interesting," she says.

"I'm pulling up to Arlene Lafontaine's house now," I say. "Just wanted you to know about Justin."

"Thanks. Call me when you leave there and let me know how it goes."

When he finally comes to the door, Hank Howard tells me essentially the same thing Justin had—though without the expensive lawyer part.

"Ain't givin' no more," he says. "Should'a got what you needed the first time. TV news says y'all don't know what you're doin' and are about to frame up somebody for it. Well . . . ain't gonna be me."

When I get back in the car and drive away, I call Reggie back.

"That was fast," she says.

"Seems he too is done cooperating," I say. "Evidently every-body's doing it."

"You have no idea," she says. "I just got off the phone with Trace's attorney and was told the same thing. His client won't be returning to Gulf County for questioning. He will not be speaking with us again. If we'd like to submit questions in writing to him, he'll see if his client is willing to answer them in writing, but no guarantees."

"From what Merrill says, Trace's life is unraveling."

"Arnie's right, be a good time to question him."

"Yes it would," I say. "Maybe we can figure something out. Merrill might be able to help us some on that end."

"Well, let it go for tonight," she says. "Kiss your wife. Hug your babies. We'll regroup in the morning. See where we go from here."

"I plan to do those very things," I say.

But a dangerous and demented man with a gun had a plan of his own—a plan that differed from mine about as much as a plan possibly could.

48

When I enter our home, no one greets me.

When I call out to my girls, none of them respond.

When I step far enough into the kitchen to see through the living room that the french doors in the back are ajar, I realize something is wrong—or could be.

I had parked beside Anna's Mustang in the driveway and passed the stroller in the mudroom on my way in, so they haven't gone for a drive or a walk.

I rush over to the back door and look out into the backyard, actually stepping out onto the porch and looking down around the lake and in the neighbors' yards.

There are no signs of them.

When I re-enter the house, I draw my weapon, hoping I'm overreacting.

Removing my phone from my pocket, I check to make sure I haven't missed any calls or texts from Anna.

There are none.

I text Dad and Verna, then Daniel and Sam, to see if they've heard from Anna and the girls.

Then I begin my search of our home.

Easing down the hallway quietly, I listen carefully, trying to detect any sound that would signal both their presence and whereabouts.

About halfway down the hall I hear the whimpering of a child and the soft incessant talking of a man.

I start to text Reggie, but since I don't know exactly what's going on and I doubt having a SWAT team outside would help, I decide against it.

As I get closer, I can tell the sounds are coming from the girls' room, which is at the end of the hall and around the corner to the right.

I start to take my shoes off so I can move even more quietly, but decide taking them off would make more noise than keeping them on and continuing to walk with them.

I thumb the safety off my Glock as I near the foyer.

I'm pretty sure I've been quiet enough to go undetected, but I'm wrong.

"Why don't you come on in here and join us, John," Chris says. "But leave your weapons out there in the hallway."

Without laying my gun down, I continue.

When I reach the end of the hallway and turn the corner, I bring up my gun, but then quickly drop it to the floor.

Inside the girls' room, Chris sits on the floor holding Taylor, his biological daughter, like she's a stranger to him, which she is. Beside him, Johanna sits crying quietly, his gun to the back of her head.

One slip of his finger, one tiny little twitch, just an inadvertent jerk, and my daughter will be dead. It doesn't even have to be intentional. A little cough or a small sneeze and the most precious little girl in the whole world to me will be as lifeless as JonBenét or Nicole or Mariah, and I will join John Ramsey, Trace Evers, and Jerry Raffield as a father who lost a daughter.

In the back corner across from them, Anna sits with her back against the wall, her wrists and ankles bound together by zip ties.

All three of my girls look relieved to see me.

"I told you to drop your gun in the hallway," Chris says.

I pivot a little and kick it back out into the hallway.

Chris looks down at Johanna. "What should daddy's punishment be for disobeying Uncle Chris, huh?"

Johanna looks up at me, her big brown frightened eyes searching mine for what to do, how to respond.

"Look at me," Chris says. "Not him. What should I do to him?"

She looks at him, but still doesn't answer.

"If you don't tell me what to do to him I'm gonna shoot him," he says.

"Timeout," she says. "He should have to go in timeout."

"Doesn't seem punitive enough," he says, "but I said I'd let you decide, didn't I? Okay, John, toss your phone and other gun over here and then we'll put you in timeout."

I do as he says, moving very slowly, then lift my hands up, palms facing out in a placating gesture.

He checks the phone to make sure it's not recording, keeping Taylor trapped in his lap and the gun to Johanna's head. Then he places the phone and gun on the floor to his right.

He's in no hurry and this take a few minutes.

"You try anything and your daughter dies first," he says.

"I know. I'm not going to try anything. Please just remove the gun from her head. It's so easy for accidents to happen with—"

"You took my daughter from me," he says. "Why shouldn't I do the same?"

I haven't taken his daughter from him, but I can understand how he sees it that way. And not for the first time lately, I am overcome with sadness and loss.

So much loss. Jerry Raffield losing Randa. Chris losing Taylor. Trace losing Mariah. John and Patsy losing JonBenét. I have been here before. Though not quite the same, losing Martin Fisher the way I had in the way I did at such an early age is a scar I've carried with me ever since.

On the floor beside Chris, my phone vibrates, and I wonder if it's Dad or someone calling me back about where Anna and the girls are.

"Chris, *your* daughter is in your lap," Anna says. "She hasn't been taken from you."

"Close the door behind you and sit on the floor with your back against it," he says.

I comply, moving very slowly and deliberately, making sure I don't do anything to make him react in any way.

"Why?" He says. "Why is she in my lap right now? Look what I had to do just to have a little time with her. Look what . . . y'all make me do just to see my own flesh and blood."

"It's not us and you know it," she says. "A judge will decide all that."

"But you're fighting for me not to see her."

"I'm trying to protect her," she says. "I'm not trying to keep her away from you. All I want is what's best for her. That's it. Given all that you've done . . . I'm sure you can understand me wanting supervision in place. I'm trying to protect *your* daughter. You have a gun inches away from her, Chris. Are you really saying—"

"He has a gun around her all the time," he says, nodding toward me.

"That's different and you know it," she says. "His is holstered or put up, never out or as close to the girls as yours is now."

"He's around her all the time. He's taken everything from me. Everything. Y'all are my family. Not his. I have nothing. Nothing. I've lost absolutely everything. Y'all have everything. I shouldn't have to walk around town like a gutter bum and watch how fuckin' happy y'all are, how y'all have everything that I once had —including my own goddamn daughter. Get so sick of seein' y'all . . ."

"Chris," Anna says. "You're in the position you're in because of choices you made, actions you took. Nothing just happened to you. John didn't take anything from you. You can have a different life than the one you have, but you have to rebuild it. It won't be quick or easy, but you can do it."

He doesn't say anything for a long moment, just seems to contemplate what she's said.

"I want my old life back," he says. "Want what we had."

My phone continues to vibrate next to Chris but he doesn't seem to notice.

Anna seems like she might be getting through to him. He's at least listening. I decide not to say anything, just let her talk to him and see what happens.

"You have to take responsibility for all you've done," she says. "That's where it starts. Then you have to work hard to rebuild, and there's no going back. There's nothing to go back to—and that's not just true of you or us, that's true of everything. Whatever was back there is long gone. There is no going back. But you can move forward. Accept responsibility. Make amends. Work on your character defects."

"How can I make amends with you?"

"It would start by putting down the gun and not holding us hostage," she says.

"I want to make everything up to you," he says. "Show you how sorry I am and how it'll be different this time. Win you back."

"That's not something you can do with a gun," she says. "Not something you can do by breaking into our home and threatening us."

"You sayin' I have a shot?" he says. "I mean with you. Could we be together again?"

"That's not a conversation we can have in this situation," she says. "You have a gun to the back of Johanna's head."

"Just to keep y'all from doing anything stupid."

"You've got me tied up."

"Just to protect you. I don't want anybody getting hurt. I don't. And I know how you are over these two. I just wanted some time with my little girl. That's not too much to ask, is it?"

"Of course not," she says, "but this isn't the way to do it."

"How else was I gonna do it?"

"By getting a job. By paying your back child support. By not stalking us. By seeing a therapist. By showing the judge you're taking the extraordinary and undeserved second chance you got and doing something positive with it. Not like this."

"I just wanted to talk. You would't talk to me if I didn't do it this way. See how you're talking to me now. That's all I wanted. That's all. You wouldn't be doing it otherwise. I just wanted to hold my kid. For her to know I'm her daddy. She's growing up so fast—and without me in her life. She needs her real father, not some fake one."

"I understand what you want," Anna says. "I truly do. But this is not the way to go about it. Period. It's the exact opposite way."

"What do you want me to do?" he asks.

"Put down the gun. Untie me. Let us go."

"I do that, your new husband's gonna put a bullet in my brain."

"No he's not."

He looks at me.

I shake my head. "I'm not going to shoot you."

"But you're going to arrest me. Just for wanting to spend a little time with my daughter. You're gonna arrest me for that and you claim to be a kind and caring person. I don't want to go back to prison."

"One step at a time," Anna says. "Put down the gun. Let the girls go. Untie me."

He seems to think about it. "Tell you what," he says, "we're gonna skip that first step, okay? But the girls can come over there with you. Give daddy a hug, Taylor."

He tries to hug her but she's trying to squirm away.

"Y'all go sit with mommy," he says.

When he lets go of Taylor, she starts to crawl toward Anna, but Johanna doesn't move.

"You can go," he says. "Go ahead. Go to .... Anna."

Removing the gun from the back of her head and pointing it toward me, he says, "See? The gun isn't pointed at you anymore. It's okay. You can go. Go to Anna."

She looks at me.

I nod. "It's okay," I say. "Go sit with Anna."

She shakes her head.

"What is it baby?" I ask.

She shakes her little head again and begins to cry.

"What is it sweetie?" I ask.

"I . . . I . . . wet . . . myself."

"It's okay," I say. "I did too. It's what we do in situations like this. Everybody does it."

"I did it too," Anna says. "It's okay, little darlin'. I promise it is."

She's mortified, my shy, modest girl, too embarrassed to move, and it makes me want to kill Chris Taunton with my bare hands. Slowly.

"I'm sorry," Chris says. "I didn't mean to scare you like that. Tell you what, I'll move. Okay? I'll move and Anna can come to you. You don't have to move."

He picks up my phone and gun and stands, still keeping his gun pointed at me.

"Come on over here with her," he says to Anna.

"Come on," Anna says to Taylor. "Let's go sit with your sissy."

Anna tries to scoot and slide over to where Johanna is in the middle of the room, but has a difficult time doing it with her ankles and wrists bound.

"Here," Chris says, and steps over, withdraws a pocket knife from his jeans and cuts the zip ties, then takes a step back so she and Taylor can get to Johanna.

Anna pulls Johanna to her, wrapping both girls in her arms and trying not to cry.

"John, let's you and me take a little walk," Chris says.

I nod. "Okay."

"Stand up slowly," he says, motioning with the gun.

I stand very slowly.

"I'll be back in a little while," I say to Johanna. "I love you. I'm so proud of you. You're such a big girl. You did so good."

She tries to smile. "Love you, Daddy. Hurry back."

"I will."

I look at Anna and our eyes lock, but neither of us says anything, and I'm sure she's thinking what I'm thinking—*Don't do anything that might set Chris off.*

"Okay," Chris says, "clasp your hands behind your head and walk down the hallway and out the back door. "Don't get too far ahead of me and don't try anything."

I do exactly as he instructs.

When we round the corner from the hallway into the living room, Dad is hiding against the wall with his nightstick, which he brings down hard on Chris's hand holding the gun.

Before the gun hits the floor, Dad brings the stick back up and strikes Chris beneath the chin, the blow snapping his head back and knocking him to the floor, my phone and backup gun skittering out of his outstretched hand and down the hallway.

I spin around and lunge onto Chris, rolling him over and cuffing him.

Still dazed, he's extremely compliant.

"Glad he finally brought you out," Dad says. "I've been waiting out here for the past twenty minutes trying to figure out how the hell to get in that room."

49

"Hate I missed the excitement," Merrill says.

We are sitting at our kitchen table, and though it's later that night, Johanna is still sitting in my lap—where she's been since we got her cleaned up after the ordeal.

Anna is next to me, Taylor sleeping on her shoulder.

Merrill is across from me and Reggie is next to him.

I have a hand on Anna's leg and the other around Johanna.

I kiss Johanna's head, as I often have over the past few hours, her soft, still-damp hair smelling of baby shampoo.

"But sounds like ol' Jack didn't need no help," he adds.

I smile. "If Chris's arm isn't broken or if he isn't missing a couple of teeth I'll be very surprised."

"Deserves much worse," Reggie says.

"Nightstick Jack," Merrill says. "Think the sheriff's got a new name."

"Will he be in a while?" Anna asks Reggie. "What all can you charge him with?"

"Burglary for breaking into your home. Assault for the threat —aggravated assault since he had a weapon. False imprisonment for holding y'all hostage. He could get a good bit of time—especially after the judge hears about his pattern of criminal behavior and past charges."

"Will he stay in jail until his trial?" she asks.

Reggie shrugs. "It's doubtful. Most don't. Bail isn't punitive. But a condition of bail will be absolutely no contact with y'all. And who knows . . . maybe he won't be able to make bail. He's broke, right? Does he have anyone who will post it for him?"

She shrugs. "Can't imagine anyone would. His mom is dead. His dad is nearly as indigent as he is and they don't speak." She looks at me. "Can you think of anyone?"

I shrug and shake my head. "No, but . . . I just don't know him or his connections that well."

Johanna stops drawing and cranes her little neck to look up at me. "Daddy, is that bad man gonna get out of jail?"

"We're working on keeping inside for a long, long time," I say, "but we'll all protect you no matter what. Do you know that? I'm not gonna let him ever get near you again. I promise."

"I know that, Daddy."

"I mean it," I say, and hug and kiss her head again.

I'm overcome with anger when I think of the barrel of Chris's gun anywhere near this precious little head.

"I know, Daddy."

"I'm so sorry I wasn't here when he first came. I wish I had been. I'm so, so, so sorry you had to go through that."

"It's okay, Daddy."

"No it's not, and I'm not going to let it happen again."

"It was my fault," Anna says. "I let my guard down for a moment and—I should've been better prepared. It won't happen again. I promise too."

"More I think about this," Merrill says to Reggie, "the more I might need you to arrest me and throw me in a cell with ol' Christopher."

Reggie looks at Johanna. "We're all going to be looking out for you. Not gonna let anything like that ever happen again."

Johanna nods. "Thank you, Sheriff Reggie."

I've been worried about Reggie. The media coverage of this case has taken a toll—both on her and her relationship with Merrick. She's joked a few times about their relationship possibly not surviving this case and I want to make sure they were only jokes. But so far I've not been able to. I make a mental note to do it the next time we're alone.

"It's my fault in more ways than one," Anna says. "I can't believe I was ever married to him—and for as long as I was . . ."

"It's not your fault in any ways," I say. "I mean it."

"It's not your fault, Anna," Johanna says.

"Don't blame yourself for bad men," Reggie says. "Life's too short. We're not responsible for . . . the actions of the sick and twisted, controlling and demented . . . Don't put that on yourself."

"She's right," I say. "Listen to her. Please. You are not to blame for anything that happened."

"Even if he does make bail," Reggie says, "which sounds doubtful, we'll be watching him like it's the only thing we have to do. If he even thinks about looking in this direction, we'll lock him up for violation of bail and he'll stay inside until trial—and then a long, long time after he's convicted."

"How about a change of subject?" Anna says.

"Sounds good," Reggie says. "Merrill, the hell you doin' home?"

"Ol' Trace pink-slipped my ass. Said my services were no longer needed, but he'll hit me up if he ever needs a body guard or PI in Florida again. Gig went longer than it was supposed to anyway. And I think he's runnin' out of money. He's overextended like a mofo, losing income right and left, and from what I gather ol' Irvin Hunter, who pulled a Houdini, has been skimming from him for years."

50

The next morning, Sam and I interview Caden Stevens.

I had to fight to use Sam, but I'm not involving her just because I think it will be good for her. I know she will be an asset. She's a great investigator and she's been studying the case, and I believe her current condition will put both Caden and his mom at ease.

We are in the interview room of the investigative division of our department. I've removed all the normal furniture and replaced it with two small comfortable couches and some age-appropriate toys.

Though Chris is still in jail, Merrill is at our house with Anna and the girls—the only way I can be here right now.

Marybeth Stevens, Caden's mom, is a small, pretty and perky young mother with shoulder length brown hair and big brown eyes. She's wearing a brightly colored summer dress and has a ribbon in her hair that matches it.

"Caden," I say, "this is Sam. Sam is a detective like me and a good friend. She's a very, very good person. She's spent her life catching bad guys and while she was doing that a couple of years back, one of them shot her. That's why she walks and talks the way she does."

He nods, darting his eyes over to glance at Sam.

"It's . . . nice . . . to meet . . . you . . . Caden," she says.

He gives her a little hesitant wave.

"The only reason we're here is because we're trying to figure out what happened to Mariah and who did it. Sam is my good friend. Mariah was one of your good friends, wasn't she?"

He nods.

"Are you sad that she's gone?"

He nods.

"Poor thing hasn't slept or eaten well since," Marybeth says. "Have you, baby?"

He shakes his head.

"The only thing that will help us find out exactly what happened and why and who did it," I say, "is the absolute truth. That's what we're asking you to tell us today. Just the truth. All the truth. Tell us everything you can and don't hold anything back."

"Just like we talked about," Marybeth says to him. "We always tell the truth. Always. And when we can help a friend we do, right?"

Caden nods. "Yes, ma'am."

"Those . . . are . . . great . . . to live . . . by," Sam says.

"What kinds of things did you and Mariah do together?" I ask.

He shrugs. "Watched . . . movies. Played games. Hung out."

I nod. "That's good. What kinds of things would you talk about when you were hanging out?"

He shrugs again. "Just stuff. I don't know. We watched her video. She sang for me."

"A private concert. That's cool."

"Yeah."

"What kind of stuff did you talk about?"

He shrugs.

"Tell him everything," Marybeth says.

"About music . . . and movies . . . and things we like to do."

"What kinds of things did Mariah like to do?"

"Sing and listen to music and skate and dance and shop and hang out with friends."

"Did Mariah have a boyfriend?" I ask.

He doesn't respond at first. Eventually, he shakes his head. "No, sir. Not . . . until . . . me."

I nod. "So y'all were boyfriend and girlfriend, not just friends?" I ask.

He nods.

"That's great. Y'all make a great couple. I'm so sorry for what happened to her."

He nods. "Me too."

"What kind of boyfriend and girlfriend stuff did you and Mariah do?" I ask.

He shrugs. "Hold hands. Talk. Text. Take pictures. Kiss. Just hang out."

I nod. "That's really great," I say.

"It was so sweet," Marybeth says. "Should've seen them. So cute. Just can't . . . Still can't believe what happened. It's devastated us all."

"Caden, did Mariah ever tell you any secrets?" I ask.

He sort of shrugs and nods at the same time.

"Like what?"

"I don't know. Just stuff. She said Brett was mean to her and his mother always took up for him."

"Did Brett play with y'all?"

"He tried a few times, but she made him leave."

"Did she say anything else about Brett or his mom, Ashley?"

"He tried to do stuff to her and his mom wouldn't stop him."

"What kind of stuff?" I ask.

He shrugs. "Boyfriend stuff."

"Do you know like what?"

He shakes his head, but says, "Like kiss her and touch her and stuff. Make her sit there and watch him play his dumb video games. Stuff like that."

"Where would he touch her?"

Again the shrug. "I don't know. Private places."

"Did he hurt her?"

He shrugs. "I don't think so. Think he just mainly annoyed her."

"Did you talk to him about it?"

"Told him to leave her alone, that I was her boyfriend and he was her brother."

"What'd he say?"

"That he wasn't her brother. That he was her boyfriend first. And would be again when we all left vacation. Might as well play Minecraft with him instead of hang out with her."

"Did you?"

"No, sir."

"Did she say anyone else touched her like a boyfriend?"

He shrugs. "No, sir."

"Did you?"

"Just a little. She wanted me to more. But Miss Nadine kept coming in."

"What did she want you to do?"

He shrugs.

Marybeth says, "I told him he didn't do anything wrong. That it's normal kid curiosity, playin' doctor and stuff like we all did. Nothin' to be ashamed of or embarrassed about."

"That's . . . exactly . . . right," Sam says.

"What did she want you to do?" I ask.

"Down there . . . stuff. Touch . . . rub."

"Had you ever done that before?" I ask.

He shakes his head. "No, sir."

"Before this vacation all his friends have been boys," Marybeth says.

"Had she?"

He nods. "That's how she knew she liked it."

"Liked what?"

"Bein' touched. Having . . . something put inside her."

"What sorts of things?"

He shrugs and glances at his mom.

She nods to him.

"A finger or a . . . something like that. Whatever was . . . around. Whatever we . . . could find."

"This is . . . difficult . . . to talk . . . about," Sam says. "You're . . . doin' so . . . good, Caden."

"Mama's proud of you, buddy," Marybeth says. "You're really helping the police with their investigation. Makes you a good citizen and a hero."

The fact that at her age Mariah was the sexually assertive one and had already had her sexuality awakened somehow makes me wonder if she was the victim of child molestation. And if so, by whom? I know it doesn't necessarily mean that, but it could.

"Did she say who else had done that to her before?" I ask.

He shakes his head.

"Is that why she was running away?" I ask.

He shrugs. "Think to get away from . . . Brett and his mom, maybe. She . . . she wanted me to go with her, but . . ." he shakes his head. "I couldn't. Couldn't leave . . . my family."

"Where was she running to?"

He shrugs. "Don't know. Just away. Back home to get her things and then . . . I don't know. She said we could stay with some of her friends or somebody. Maybe her grandparents— think she really wanted to meet them. Or Miss Nadine. She said she'd take us in. "

"*We?*"

"Me and her."

"I thought you weren't going?"

"I wasn't. I didn't. She just wanted me to."

51

"Well?" Reggie says.

Sam and I are in her office.

It's just the three of us. Arnie and Keisha are in Atlanta working surveillance with GBI on Trace, Ashley, and Irvin. Jessica is going over the DNA results and will have a report for us soon.

It's later that afternoon. Sam is tired and I need to get her home soon, but she insisted we meet with Reggie first.

Reggie watched the interview video while I took Sam to lunch.

"He . . . seemed to be . . . tellin' . . . the . . . truth," Sam says.

I nod. "I agree."

"Me too," Reggie says.

"I . . . found it a . . . little . . . odd," Sam says, "how . . . cooperative his . . . mother . . . was."

"I did too," I say. "We're living in a post-forensics and investigative techniques world. She'd have to know Caden was a suspect. Is she that naive or is it something else?"

"That's . . . what . . . I won . . .der . . . ed," Sam says.

"Just seemed like a good citizen, eager to help to me," Reggie says.

"Maybe so," I say. "But you'd at least think she'd have a lawyer."

Sam nods.

"Before I forget," Reggie says. "Got a call from GBI. Still haven't gotten anywhere with the drive-by but they're fairly certain Little Swag or operatives acting on his behalf are responsible."

I nod.

"Means I'm tellin' you there's nothin' to tell you, but . . . just thought I'd tell you."

I nod. "Thank you."

"Okay," she says. "Back to . . . So we thinkin' maybe Mariah was a victim of molestation?"

"It's . . . possible," Sam says. "Sometimes . . . kids . . . are more . . . sexual . . . earlier than . . . average and . . . it's not . . . the result . . . of molestation."

"We need to talk to her pediatrician," Reggie says, making herself a note on the pad on her desk. "If she had been molested and it's related to her murder . . . it'd most likely be Trace or Irvin, right?"

I nod.

"Or Brett," Sam says.

Reggie shakes her head. "Crime's too sophisticated for a ten-year-old boy."

"Hate . . . to . . . sound . . . like . . . certain members . . . of the . . . Boulder . . . po . . . lice . . . de . . . part . . . ment, but . . . Brett commits . . . the . . . crime . . . and Ash . . . ley covers . . . it . . . up."

Reggie nods. "Now *that's* possible. I can buy that. Still think it's more likely Trace or Irvin, but . . . this scenario is at least possible."

A tap on Reggie's open door and Jessica appears.

"We've got him," she says.

"Who?" Reggie asks.

Jessica comes the rest of the way into the office, standing near where Sam and I are sitting across from Reggie's desk.

"The DNA results," she says, holding up a sheaf of papers. "There are only two findings that are really relevant. Everything else is just what you'd expect."

"Well, let's hear it."

"The ropes used on Mariah," she says. They only have Ashley's and Trace's DNA on them. No one else's."

Reggie nods. "That's—"

"Mariah's, of course, but I mean they were on her, so figured you knew that."

"They did it," Reggie says. "We follow the evidence and that's what the evidence says."

"Evidence says *he* did it," Jessica says. "I mean, sure she could've been involved or helped him cover it up, but . . . he definitely did it."

"What makes you say that?" Reggie asks. "What else did they find?"

"The stains that looked like dried semen on Mariah's bedsheets, well it was. It was Trace's semen. Trace left traces of himself in his own daughter's bed."

"No wonder he quit cooperating," Reggie says. "Fired Merrill and isn't willing to come back for another interview. He did it. We have enough for a warrant now. We're gonna actually be able to clear this thing. Maybe the surveillance will turn up additional evidence, but we have enough to make an arrest now."

We nod.

"And . . . it fits . . . with the other . . . evidence . . . you . . . have," Sam says.

"Fuck yeah," Reggie says. "We're gonna get a child molester and murderer off the street. That feels good. Damn good."

Sam is about to say something else, but Reggie's phone rings and she snatches it up.

While she's listening, she points at me, nods, though she has an alarmed expression on her face, and mouths *Go home. Now.*

I jump up as she returns the receiver to its cradle.

"Chris made bail," she says. "I don't know how, but . . . we'll take care of things here and figure out what to do about him, but for now . . . go be with your family."

52

I have an eventful drive home. At least mentally.

The twenty miles or so between the sheriff's department in Port St. Joe and our home in Wewa is, like most of the rural highways in North Florida, straight, flat, and largely empty, which gives me plenty of time to think.

After telling Anna what's going on and making sure she and Daniel are both armed, I turn my mind to the most pressing questions of the moment, as Sam sleeps in the passenger seat beside me.

Who would've posted bail for Chris and why? If he has not friends or family, no resources of his own, how would he get someone to do it for him? Was it someone who he knows too much about, someone concerned he'd use evidence on them to cut a deal? If not, what other motive could there be?

And then it hits me.

I know who it is and why—or think I do, and if I do, if I'm right, then it can be only one of two possible motives, and I don't know which one is frightening.

I call Merrill, tell him what's going on, and ask him to go see if he can persuade the bail bondsman into revealing who posted

Chris's bail—something I'm reasonably confident not only because Merrill does skip traces for him but because of how persuasive Merrill can be.

With that underway, I turn my attention to what Caden said during our interview with him, what it means, the fact that Trace's DNA was found in Mariah's bed, and I begin to see how the murder of Mariah might have taken place and what the various evidence we've uncovered could mean in terms of confirming and proving it.

When I get home, I hug and hold my girls and then help them pack.

"Who's wants to go on a little vacation?" I say.

"And stay in a hotel?" Johanna asks.

"Yes."

"So we'll still be in the same room with you and Anna?"

"Yes."

"And we can jump on the bed?"

"Absolutely," I say. "That's what hotel beds are for."

"I do. I do."

"We'll see if Papa Jack and Verna and Uncle Merrill can go too."

"Yay. And Za too?"

"Sure."

"How about Sam and Daniel?"

"I'll ask them, but I think Sam may not quite be ready for this much fun and excitement yet."

After booking three random hotel rooms in Mexico Beach under Verna's previous name and paying with her credit card that still has that name on it, and getting Anna and the girls settled into our room and Dad and Verna in their adjoining one, Merrill and I get back on Highway 98 and head west to put my theory to the test.

"If we been lookin' all this time and she right here in our backyard . . ." Merrill says.

"I could be wrong."

"Not according to Keller you ain't."

Keller Branch is the bail bondsman who bonded out Chris and according to his records the person who put up the money for it was Nancy Drury.

Nancy Drury is an alias for Randa Raffield. She's not in some non-extradition country sippin' on sex on the beaches. She's right here.

And I think she's at her dad's.

It would explain why he keeps calling me to check in, to find out what I know or if I have a lead on where she is. He hasn't been looking for her, he's been trying to protect her. It would also explain how she was able to vanish so completely and how she would have been able to handle Daniel—both of which she would have needed help with.

And now we're racing over to Seaside to see if I'm right.

"Even if I'm right about her putting up the bail money," I say, "I could be wrong about her being with her dad."

"We'a soon find out," Merrill says.

"She's my daughter, John," Jerry Raffield says. "I had to help her, had to take her in and . . . I was just so glad to have her back in my life. I . . . I thought she was dead for so long . . . to get her back was like having a child come back from the dead. Who wouldn't want that?"

I understand what he's saying and why he would do it— something I wouldn't have nearly as well before I had Johanna.

Thinking of Johanna reminds me of Chris holding his gun to her precious little head and fills me with a deep red rage that makes me want to kill him.

The fire of my rage is extinguished by my overwhelming

desire to be with her, to have her in my arms, to be there protecting her than over here chasing down Jerry's daughter.

"This whole time," he adds, "I—you'll appreciate this—the entire time she's been here with me I keep thinking of the parable of the prodigal son and what the father said, 'My son who was dead is alive again.'"

I nod. "I get it. I do. But we still have to take her in. Is she here?"

He shakes his head. "She's not back yet."

"From?"

"Over your way," he says. "I tried to get her not to go, but . . . I can't get her to do or not do anything she doesn't want to. I begged her."

"She went to hire Keller Branch to post bail for Chris Taunton," I say.

He nods. "I gathered it was something like that."

"What else was she going to do?" I ask. "She should've been back quite a while ago."

"I don't want to think about it," he says, "but . . . I'm afraid she might be planning to do something to him. You've got to stop her. Please. She'd be doing it for you, for what she feels like she owes you. She'd see it as settling her account with you. Please stop her. Protect her from herself. Please."

A fter having the Walton County Sheriff's Department take Jerry into custody, I feel sad and guilty.

Jerry had lost Randa and it devastated him, but then he got her back. Now he is losing her again—and not just her, but a big part of his life as well.

Now Merrill and I are racing back toward Wewa to try to stop Randa from killing Chris.

The irony is not lost on us.

"I can drive slower," Merrill says. "You could not call Reggie about sending a deputy over to check on him. Just seems surreal to be tryin' to save the bastard who had a gun to Johanna's head yesterday. And tried to have you killed not so long ago."

"It is," I say. "Surreal. But . . . don't look at it as saving *him* so much as catching *her*. Just finishing what we set out to do."

"But we can still do that *after* she puts one in Chris's brainpan."

"I know," I say. "But . . . I can't just let her kill him."

"Only way that makes any sense is if you want him for yourself—or your best friend and Johanna's godfather."

I smile. "Sorry."

He laughs and shakes his head. "How many times you wanted his sorry ass dead just in the past twenty-four hours?"

"Too many to count," I say.

"But when an opportunity arises for that very thing to happen your ass is workin' to stop it."

"Yeah."

"Don't ever change, babe," he says. "Don't ever fuckin' change."

I call Reggie and explain the situation to her and ask her to have a deputy check on Chris and stay with him until we get there.

When I'm off the phone, Merrill says, "Let me ask you somethin'. You feel bad for having Jerry arrested, don't you?"

I nod. "I do. Whatta you want me to say? I'm sorry, but I do. Guy got his daughter back from the dead."

"Made a deal with the devil to do it," he says. "And the devil is his daughter."

"She may or may not be the devil, but she *is* his daughter."

"Like I said, don't ever change, babe. Whatever you do, don't ever change."

53

The small house is dark and quiet.

I'm set up on the front door in the living room. Merrill is set up on the back door in the kitchen.

We're in Chris's tiny, dilapidated rental on Second Street waiting to see if Randa shows.

It's late. We've been waiting a while.

All around us the town has shut down for the night. There is no traffic on Second Street and only the occasional, lone vehicle on Main.

Earlier, Reggie moved Chris to a secure, secret location. Since we arrived, we've just been waiting.

Reggie and a deputy are hidden at each end of the street.

I shouldn't be in here. Neither should Merrill. But I reminded Reggie she owed me for what I had done for her mom. I basically blackmailed her because I had to be here when Randa walked in —and because I knew Merrill needed to be after she stole Daniel right out from underneath him.

Chris's mostly empty, about-to-collapse little wooden house is a sad reflection of his own implosion. Barren, hollowed out, on borrowed time.

It smells of neglect, of the years-old, baked-in sweat and cigarette smoke of previous tenants, of the mildew of damp, rotting boards, and the hint of a septic system not working properly.

It's the fringe smell of desperation and decay, and indicates just how far the once hot shot Tallahassee attorney has fallen.

I'm missing my girls so much I'm about to tell Merrill we should call it a night, when I hear the unmissable metallic ticks and scratches of a lock being picked. They're coming from the back door.

I move across the small living room and position myself against the wall next to the opening to the kitchen.

In another few moments, the lock is picked and the back door creaks open.

And Randa is following the beam of a small penlight into the room.

She's only taken a few steps inside the kitchen when Merrill steps from behind the antique GE refrigerator and places the barrel of his gun to the back of her head.

"Drop it," he says.

"You're surrounded," I say.

"Okay," she says and drops both her light and the murder kit she's carrying.

I snap on the bare bulb overhead light as Merrill subdues her and zip ties her wrists behind her back.

She smiles when she sees us. "Should've known," she says. "Thought I could be in and out before you even realized I was the one who posted bail."

I withdraw a pair of latex gloves from my pocket and put them on. Stepping over to where her penlight and small leather bag are, I pick them up.

A quick glance in the bag reveals a small pistol, syringes, and several small vials with no identification on them.

"Seriously," she says. "No way, y'all've already had a hearing to—"

"Merrill was able to obtain the information on his own," I say.

"I owed you one," Merrill says from behind her.

"You did at that," she says. "At least one."

I place her bag and light on the leaning lemon formica table, take off my gloves, and pull out my phone to call for a deputy to take her into custody.

"Don't suppose you'd give a girl a head start," she says. "I was here to do you a favor after all."

I shake my head and smile at her.

"I'll tell you who killed Mariah," she says.

"I already know," I say.

54

"Mariah's murder was what a lot of people thought JonBenét's was," I say.

Arnie and Keisha are back from Atlanta. They, along with me, Reggie, Jessica, and the district attorney—a middle-aged man named Houston Reynolds—are in Roger Garrett's rental house one last time.

We're here at my request. We were supposed to be meeting in Reggie's office to go over the case against Trace Evers and to coordinate with Dekalb County on his arrest, but I've asked them back out here to hear me out during a crime scene walkthrough before we do.

"Many if not most people, especially early on, thought JonBenét's death was unintentional and that the crime scene was staged, part of an elaborate coverup, but you only have to look at JonBenét's autopsy report to know that what that poor child suffered through was a horrific, brutal assault and murder. Unlike, Mariah, JonBenét had defensive wounds. She was struggling against her killer, fighting for her life. We see none of that with Mariah."

"You're sayin' we're dealing with staging at this crime scene," Reynolds says. "It's part of a cover-up to hide what really happened?"

I nod.

Houston Reynolds is a soft, pudgy, sweaty man with a sparse halo of light brown hair and squarish glasses that keep sliding down his nose.

"Even if there was some staging involved," Keisha says, "Mariah was sexually assaulted. That's what was being covered up."

I shake my head. "I don't think so."

"You sayin' the notes and ropes were all part of a staged crime scene?" Arnie asks. "I'm tryin' to follow you."

We're standing in the main floor great room, each of us holding notebooks and pens and crime scene photos and notes and the autopsy report.

"Was she not really running away?" Reggie says. "The note is in her handwriting."

"No, she was," I say. "Only the ropes were part of the staging."

"But the ransom note," Keisha says. "If there was staging, that's part of it."

"A jury is never gonna follow all this," Reynolds says.

"Let's start with the runaway note," I say. "I believe Mariah wrote it and had planned to run away."

"Then why have a ransom note? And if you're gonna leave the ransom note, why not remove the runaway note?"

"I don't think he saw it," I say. "Let's walk up to the room Mariah was staying in."

They agree and we do, Reynolds bringing up the rear, breathing heavily and sweating even more.

"Mariah was going to run away because, as she put it, Brett and Ashley were being mean to her. I believe that's why—well, that and how overbearing and overprotective Trace could be."

"Not because her daddy was sexually molesting her?" Keisha says.

I shake my head. "I don't think he was."

We are all standing in Mariah's room, fanned out around the bed.

"Then who?" she says. "*His* semen was found in her bed. You saying he was framed?"

"No. It was his semen and he left it here—but with Ashley, not Mariah. Ashley told me that she and Trace have sex all the time. She's his bottom, his submissive. He takes her when he wants to. They try to do it in every room in the house. I think at some point during their stay, Trace and Ashley had sex in this bed—or against it. Maybe while the kids were downstairs watching a movie with Nadine or eating, or down at the beach. I think that's why his DNA was found on the bedsheets in here."

"But Mariah was sexually assaulted," Keisha says. "It's like you're ignoring that."

Reynolds nods and says, "What's easier to buy, that Trace and . . . ah, Ashley had sex on this bed and just happen to leave DNA evidence, or that because of the sexual assault evidence that he was molesting her and that's why it's there?"

"And it's not just that," Keisha says. "Look at how he sexualized her in that video they made together and how he acts in general—like in his other videos. They're like a confession."

"I don't think she's sexualized in any way in the video they made together," I say. "It's sweet and fun. Looks like home movies of a dad and daughter who really like each other. But would you accept my explanation for his DNA in this bed if we knew he didn't molest her?"

She nods and Reynolds shrugs.

"Remember that the vaginal trauma Mariah suffered didn't take place at the time of her death, but twenty-four to thirty-six hours *prior* to her death."

"Yeah, he assaulted her earlier and killed her to cover it up," Keisha says.

"The party the night before falls within that timeframe," I say. "And I think that's when it happened. Mariah and Caden Stevens, the boy from next door, were sweet on each other and kissed and experimented a little sexually. He said she asked him to stick things in her—like his finger and other objects around. Nadine watched them closely, but when she wasn't looking I think they were playing doctor the way kids sometimes do. My guess is there's an object in this room that he used that has her DNA on it that is sharp enough to cause the injuries detailed in the autopsy."

I turn and look at the little desk with the open stapler on it. They follow my gaze.

"Something like this," I say.

With my gloved hand, I lift the narrow metal pusher rod and follow spring.

"We can ask Caden about it and have it tested to know for sure," I say, "but if it's not this it'll be something like it."

"You sayin' Caden killed her to cover it up?" Jessica asks.

"That's certainly not a bad theory," I say. "Neither is Brett killing her because of it—out of jealousy or because she wouldn't let him do the same thing, but . . . I don't think it's either one of those. I don't think the relatively mild vaginal trauma Mariah suffered has anything to do with her murder."

I withdraw a plastic evidence bag from my coat pocket and drop the staple pusher into it and place it back on the table.

"If that's true," Reggie says, "and it makes sense, then it changes the motive for the murder, doesn't it?"

"Then we're back to kidnapping and ransom," Keisha says.

"But why tie her up like that and kill her?" Arnie says. "It makes no sense."

"Brett said he thought he saw a man with no face pass by his door that night," I say. "I think that was our would-be kidnapper and that he was wearing a mask."

"Who was it?" Arnie asks.

"Who could it have been?" I say. "Who would need a mask and a taser? Who would know Trace always carries two-hundred-and-fifty-thousand dollars in cash at all times? Who would write such a condescending and racist ransom note? Whose handwriting couldn't be eliminated as a suspect based on his handwriting sample?"

Reggie says, "Hank Howard, Jr., Ashley's brother."

"He and his mother are so bitter that Trace won't give them some of his money. They live in abject poverty and resent Trace. I heard Hank tell his mother he had been working on something, that his ship was about to come in. I think he had overheard Ashley talking about the cash that Trace always carries at some point and decided if Trace wasn't going to let Ashley give her family some of his money, he'd just take it. His prints were all over the house, not just on the first floor like most of the other party guests. My guess is he scoped out the house the night of the party—and even tore a piece of paper out of Trace's song journal when he saw it on his bedside table. Probably hoped Trace would know it was an inside job and not call the police."

"How do you explain no taser marks on the victim's body?" Reynolds asks.

"He never tased her," I say. "My guess is he placed the note down—didn't even see her note. No telling what all he didn't see with the mask on. And he tased the pillows Mariah had put under her covers to make it look like she was sleeping. He pulls the covers back, sees she's not there. Panics and runs out, leaving the note, the blast plate, and one of the probes behind."

"So he didn't kill her?" Reggie asks.

I shake my head. "I don't think so."

"Then who?"

"Who would help her run away?" I ask. "Who would want to

help her and hurt Trace? Who would have to take her iPod so their texting wouldn't be discovered? Who would use Mariah's own mom to manipulate her—and be in the best position to do it? Who would bribe her with getting her ears pierced? Who would Mariah let in the house that night?"

"Who?" Reynolds says.

55

"I know you didn't mean to kill her," I say.

I'm in Deidra's small office in Myra House, this place where she does so much good for so many people.

I don't like being here. Not for the reason I am.

To Reynolds question of *who* I responded that no one wanted Mariah away from Trace more than Deidra did, no one wanted to surprise her folks with their granddaughter, some living piece of their daughter, more than she did. I think Mariah mentioned wanting to run away, and Deidra not only encouraged her but told her she'd help her. My guess is she took her folks to Helen for the Fourth as part of her alibi, that she invented an emergency at Myra House and instead of going there, drove to Cape San Blas instead to get Myra's daughter. She said she had to be back to Myra House the second day of their vacation—the Fourth—but Sandy let it slip that Deidra had been away for the entire time, said the place fell apart without her there.

She went to Cape San Blas to get Mariah and took the picture of her with Myra and Mariah to bolster their connection and Mariah's trust. She also took the earrings to show her what her new life could be like. She knew she had to explain why her prints would be on items at a crime scene 300 miles away from where she was supposed to be, so she volunteered the info when I first spoke to her, telling me she had given Mariah the picture and her mom had given Mariah the earrings at an earlier time, but Rhonda Baxley's prints weren't on the earrings and she told me she hadn't seen Mariah since Myra died.

"You didn't, did you?" I say. "Mean to kill her."

She still doesn't say anything.

"I don't think you did. I think Mariah changed her mind about running away. Did Caden not being willing to go make her want to stay?"

Tears fill her eyes, but she still doesn't speak.

"I keep thinking of how Mariah died," I say. "A single blow to the back of the head. And the way she was tied up afterwards—as part of the staging to make it look like something else. You did that to get back at Trace, didn't you? To cause him even more grief and pain. I just keep remembering how there were no abrasions or bruises where the ropes touched Mariah's skin. That's because she was already dead when you tied her up."

She nods.

After answering Reynolds' question and laying out my theory for everyone at the rental house in Stars Haven, Reynolds had responded that it was far too complicated to get a conviction and that he wouldn't bring it to trial. So I asked Reggie if I could try to get Deidra to confess and she said she was going to suggest it if I hadn't.

Which is why I'm here now.

After mirandizing Deidra and letting her know I'm recording our conversation, I began laying out the evidence against her and what I think happened, piece by piece, line by line, slowly, methodically.

It seems to be working.

"The most negative information about Trace came from you —someone who blames him for her sister's death—and Chance

Hill, a habitual offender still serving time long after Trace is out and doing well. Perhaps it was easier for everyone to believe —us and the media because Trace is African-American, an ex-con, and has a certain image as a rapper, but . . . I don't believe he's the monster you think he is. Anyway, Mariah comes down stairs to unlock the door for you and Caden. But Caden's not there, is he? It's just you. You give her the gifts. She thanks you and slips them in her backpack. You ask if she's ready. She says she has to wait for Caden. And when you tell her Caden can't go . . . what happens?"

"I . . . I . . . started thinking about what I was risking," she says. "Everything. Everything—including this place and the work I do here—to save her and . . . she doesn't want to go now because some little boy that she just met won't go with her."

"Did she say she was going over to Caden's or just back up to bed? Or did she threaten to wake her dad? Did you grab her? Did she trip? Fall? What did she hit her head on?"

I think of the huge bronze sea turtle near the door, how much its beak-like mouth matches Mariah's head wound, and how the lab was testing it at this very moment.

She doesn't say anything.

I wait.

She doesn't say anything else or respond in any way for a quite a while.

I continue to wait.

Eventually, more tears appear in her eyes, crest, then stream down her cheeks.

"It was an accident," she says finally.

I nod.

"I would never intentionally do anything to hurt anyone, but especially that poor little motherless angel who had been through so much. I was trying to help her, to save her. I was doing what I thought Myra would have done. Acting for her. There's no way she wouldn't have gone and gotten her daughter out of that . . . No way I couldn't do it for her."

"I know," I say, continuing to nod in ways that I hope are understanding and encouraging.

"She just fell. Fell and hit her head. I was reaching for her, trying to get her not to walk away, but . . . I didn't push her or trip her or . . . anything. It happened so fast. She just hit her head on that ridiculous bronze sea turtle and . . . She was there, alive one instant, and in the next she was gone."

From down the hallway I can hear the women whose lives she's saving talking and laughing and interacting with Frank Morgan.

"What then?" I ask. "You grab her up. Carry her to her room and . . . get the idea to make it look like something other than what it was, maybe frame Trace in the process. You know about Trace tying women up from your sister. Myra used to read about it and practice it in front of you, didn't she? You told me she did. Did she talk to you about it, get you to tie her up for practice? Did you see the ropes on the landing or in the bathroom or were you brazen and committed enough to slip into Trace's room and get them?"

She nods. "His room. They were out. I knew they would be. Partying the way they do."

"But you couldn't bring yourself to leave Mariah naked, could you? You undercut your own staging by putting her swimsuit on her and tying her up over it. Then, and this is most telling of all, you lovingly wrap her in a blanket to cover her and lay her under the bed."

She nods.

"But you forgot the gifts were in Mariah's backpack as you slip out into the night and drive back to Helen, didn't you? What time did you get back—just a little before your parents knock on your door with the news that your niece is dead?"

She nods again.

"When I came to see you, I was here mostly to talk to you about Trace," I say. "You really weren't even on our radar, but you gave me your alibi and the story explaining why your prints were going to be found on the picture frame and earrings without me asking."

"After it happened . . . I thought . . . maybe some good could come of it. Maybe I could punish him for what he did to Myra. I don't know . . . something just sort of took over inside me and . . . I became a woman on a mission, so focused, so brave, so . . . it was like it wasn't me. It's hard to explain."

"I looked into your sister's death," I say. "So did Frank. Trace didn't murder her. Didn't have it done. It really was what it looked like—an accidental overdose."

"He took her from me—accident or not."

"The way you took Mariah from him," I say.

Her eyes widen in devastating recognition and she gasps.

We are silent for what seems like a long while.

"I do so much good," she says. "And have for years now. My whole life is—this is my whole life. Saving the lives of battered women, giving them a different life than what they—than the brutal hell they've always known. And this—an accident, a split-second freak accident—is what I'm gonna be known for."

I don't point out that she was wrong to be where she was in the first place and that if she hadn't been attempting to essentially kidnap her niece none of this would've happened.

"What's gonna happen to me?" she asks.

"That's up to you," I say. "But we've spoken to the district attorney and convinced him it was an accident. If you'll cooperate and plead guilty, you'll get manslaughter."

She nods and thinks about it.

"You'd still have a life," I say.

"That's more than Myra and Mariah," she says, "and more than I deserve."

56

"It was an accident, John," Frank Morgan says.

"I know."

We are standing outside Myra House.

A Dekalb County Sheriff's deputy has just taken Deidra into custody—something both of us found difficult to watch. She is guilty of obstruction and a variety of other charges related to breaking into Trace's rented house and staging the crime scene, but it is difficult to find her criminally responsible for Mariah's death.

"She shouldn't serve any time at all for an accident."

"I know what you're saying," I say. "And I made that argument to the DA, argued that Hank should get far more time than she does, but . . . think about all she did afterward. If she hadn't tried to frame Trace and Ashley . . . If she had called an ambulance instead of staging it to look like a murder committed by someone inside the house that night . . . but she didn't."

He shakes his head and frowns. "You have any idea how much good she does here?"

"I do."

Through the windows, around curtains and in between

blinds, the women of Myra House watched as their heroine and savior was taken away—and continue to watch the two of us now.

"This place can't survive without her."

"I think it can."

"How?"

"You," I say.

"Me?"

"She told me she was going to ask you to run it while she's away."

His eyes show just how appealing he finds that idea.

"Really?" he says. "Me, huh? I . . . I guess I could. How long do you think she'll be gone?"

I shrug. "Probably less than two years."

He nods. "I could do that, yeah. I'll need to get a female partner to help make sure the women feel comfortable, but . . . I could . . . run the place."

"That's great," I say. "And Anna and I will help in any way we can."

And then it hits me.

"You know . . ." I add. "Ida Williams would be a great help. I bet she'd be happy to help you."

He nods. "Probably be good for her too."

I smile. "Yes, it would. No doubt about it."

"At least tell me Hank Howard is going to get more time than Deidra. At least tell me that."

I nod. "Looks like it. The fact that he broke in with a weapon. Doesn't look like he's going to be able to make bail either, so it looks like he'll sit in jail while awaiting trial."

"Good. That's where he needs to be."

We are quiet a moment, and I notice just how much better—healthier and more vibrant—Frank looks than before he started helping out here at Myra House.

"Does Trace know?" he asks.

I nod.

While giving Deidra some time to tell her parents what had happened and what was about to happen and to get a few things in order, I had driven over to Trace's.

I found Trace all alone in his crumbling kingdom. No family. No posse. No bodyguards.

Nadine had resigned and moved out.

He and Ashley had broken up and she and Brett had moved out.

He is hemorrhaging money and losing all his income and can no longer afford to employ friends and bodyguards.

But he didn't seem to care.

He is broken and grief-stricken and seems to prefer to be alone.

"You know why we broke up?" he had asked me when we were talking about Ashley.

I shook my head, though I could probably have guessed.

"Neither of us could be completely certain that the other one didn't do it," he said. "You can't be with someone who thinks you could've murdered your child any more than you could be with someone you think could have murdered your child. And it turns out I was right about her racist piece of shit brother. Can't believe she let that sorry motherfucker know how much cash I carry. Hell, maybe she was in on it. See? I can't be sure she wasn't."

"We asked him," I said. "He says it was just him."

"Well . . ."

I didn't say anything, just waited.

"Can't believe that bitter bitch was gonna take my kid away from me in the middle of the night," he says, "but . . . I'm so glad she wasn't . . . that . . . it was an accident and she wasn't raped and didn't suffer."

I nod. "Me too. So glad."

"My life's still over," he said. "And not just because part of the world will always think I did it or had something to do with it, but because . . . biggest part of me died when she did. Don't . . want . . . no life now."

"What'd he say?" Frank asks now.

I tell him.

"Well," he says, "I guess I better get back in there and reassure all these ladies about their futures and the fate of Myra House."

57

I'm near Columbus on my way home when my phone rings.

I'm in the middle of contemplating what I do, how I approach justice, how I apply the law and how I justify it to myself.

It bothers me that Deidra will serve two years in prison for an accident while Sylvia won't serve a single second for several cold-blooded homicides.

That reminds me that I still haven't had to interact with Sylvia Summers, Reggie's mom, since telling Reggie I would keep her secret. It will happen eventually, but it's fine with me that it hasn't happened yet.

I wonder if my involvement in each case, even though in very different capacities, makes me a hypocrite. I conclude that it does —especially when I factor in what I did in regards to Verna and her role in the Janet Leigh Lester case.

It occurs to me that I apply the law and justice just as arbitrarily and inconsistently as our justice system, and it makes me equally parts ashamed and determined to do something about it.

It's late—one-thirty or so in the morning—and I don't recognize the number the call is coming from, but I answer it.

"Why didn't you come tell me?" Nadine says. "You were up here. You told everybody else, but I had to hear it on the TV. I was her mother—the closest thing that poor child had to one. Why wouldn't you tell me?"

When I didn't find Nadine at Trace's, I made no attempt to track her down to tell her about Mariah in person like I should have. I was tired and drained and all I wanted to do was rush back to be with Anna and the girls—especially given everything that had happened—but I was wrong not to tell her face to face.

"I should have," I say. "You're right. I'm sorry. I thought I'd be able to talk to you at Trace's and when you weren't there . . . I just . . . I'm very sorry."

"Well . . ."

"I'm truly sorry. I know she was like your own daughter. It was . . . I should have."

"Well, you can tell me now," she says. "Tell me what really happened, not that TV news crap."

I tell her everything I can.

"So my baby didn't suffer," she says. "Wasn't . . . messed with . . . That's . . . Thank you, Jesus. Oh, Lord, I'm so relieved to hear that. Thank you, Jesus. And John. Thank you, John."

It doesn't feel right for me to say *thank you*, so I don't say anything. But I am very glad to give her the somewhat comforting news that it was an accident.

"Now that I know for sure that boy ain't done this terrible thing," she says. "I may go back to work for him. He's got no one else right now. No daughter. No girlfriend. No stepson. No manager—even ol' Irvin left him. I know Trace doesn't have a child for me to take care of, but . . . right now he's the one needin' takin' care of. He can be my child."

"He'd be lucky to have a mom like you," I say.

"He's basically a good man," she says. "He really is. Sometimes he's a lost little boy, but . . . mostly he's a decent human being. Can you believe all the stuff the media has been saying about him? Easier for everyone to believe about a young black man like him."

"Maybe," I say. "Probably. But . . . don't forget what was reported, perceived, and believed about John Ramsey—a rich middle-aged white man."

"Guess you're right."

"But you're right about what Trace needs," I say. "You're exactly what he needs right now."

"I may not even wait until the mornin'," she says. "I may go back over there right now. He's a night owl so I'll know he'll be up. I could cook him some middle-of-the-night breakfast. That's his favorite."

"I think you should," I say.

"I think I will," she says, then thanks me again and ends the call.

58

"So she confessed?" Anna whispers.

It's the middle of the night. We're in bed. The baby monitor is off. Our girls are asleep in the room with us, their beds at angles around ours.

I nod. "Seemed to need to."

The room is night-light dim and breezy because of the box fan and window unit.

"Think it was a real unburdening," I add.

"I bet."

Johanna turns in her bed, tossing her covers about, and I lean up to check on her.

When I lie back down, Anna asks, "How long you think they'll sleep in here?"

"Is twenty-eight too old?"

She laughs and says, "I adore you, John Jordan."

"Adore you more, Mrs. Jordan."

I reach up and touch her face, tracing her features with my finger.

"I was thinking at least until Chris is sentenced," I say. "If that's okay with you."

"That's absolutely okay with me, but I don't think Chris is going to be a problem anymore—even before he's sentenced."

"Hope you're right," I say. "But I can't say I share your optimism."

"Do you really think Randa was going to kill him?" she asks.

I nod.

"Why?" she asks.

"I think maybe we've become her woes," I say.

"Huh?"

"I think she cares about us—our family, Merrill, Daniel, Merrick, Sam. Think she thinks under different circumstances she might be in our friend group."

"*Really?*"

I shrug. "I don't know. It's just an impression."

"She'd make an interesting addition to the Scooby Gang," she says.

"That she would."

"Have I told you how glad I am you're home?" she says.

"Have I told you how glad I am *to be home*?" I ask.

"I'm a little surprised Susan didn't insist on getting Johanna after what happened," she says.

"She wanted to," I say. "But Johanna told her she wanted to stay, that she felt safe. Susan felt reassured by the twenty-four-hour armed protection too. She knows Dad, Daniel, Merrill, you, Reggie—nobody would let anything happen to her, that it's not just me."

"I still can't believe he did that," she says. "Still can't believe I was ever married to him."

"You weren't married to *him*," I say. "Not that person. Even if the seeds of self-destruction were in him back then, they were just seeds. Took a lot of nurturing and watering and weeding of them for him to become what he has."

"It's . . . just so humiliating—all of it, the affairs, the deceit, the deterioration. It's really done a number on my self-esteem," she says.

"I'm so sorry," I say. "I hate that it has. Want to do anything I can to help with that."

"You do," she says. "Every second of every day."

"He is no reflection on you," I say.

"Like I say, I don't think he's going to be an issue anymore."

Before I can say anything else, my phone vibrates and lights up on the nightstand. It's Reggie, which at three-thirty-seven in the morning can't be good.

"Hey," I say.

"You back?" she asks.

"I am."

"How long you been?"

"Twenty minutes maybe. Why? What's up?"

"Randa is still in custody," she says. "I just checked. Has been since you arrested her three nights ago. So it can't have been her."

"What can't?"

"We've just found Chris," she says. "He's been murdered."

START BLOOD STONE NOW!

BLOOD STONE CHAPTER 1

I was sitting on a barstool in Scarlett's trying to act less drunk than I was when Frank Morgan walked in.

It was 1988, the one hundredth anniversary of the Jack the Ripper case, and my third year in Atlanta.

A small crowd of regulars were spread around the bar. George Michael's Father Figure was on the jukebox, but I seemed to be the only one listening. A chilly October wind whistled outside and found cracks and crevices to enter Scarlett's and make her cold and drafty.

Behind me on a small table in the back corner were textbooks I was supposed to be studying, but I was finding it difficult to focus.

I had stepped over to the bar to ask Susan for a kiss and another vodka cranberry, which she was busy making because she didn't know about the two I had before I arrived, or the one her Aunt Margaret slipped me when she wasn't looking.

Margaret, like me, was a functioning alcoholic—though I wasn't sure how well either of us was actually functioning. Of course, functioning is a relative term, and addicts like us love few things as much as equivocation.

Margaret used not to drink as much as she does now. At least that's what I'd been told. But that was back before—before she'd lost the reasons not to. Before Laney Mitchell, the love of her life, died and left her alone with the Gone with the Wind-themed bar they had started together during happier times.

Like Margaret herself, Scarlett's had fallen on hard times, the faded and dust-covered book-and-movie memorabilia more sad than anything else.

Susan handed me my drink and before taking so much as the first sip I knew it would be heavy on the cranberry and light on the vodka.

"Thanks," I said, adding, "Wait" when she turned away to open a bottle of Bud for the old gray regular across the way.

"What?"

"You forgot my kiss."

"Oh. Sorry."

She bounced back over, and placing both palms on the bar, pushed herself up and kissed me.

When I tried to respond with a similar energy and enthusiasm I turned my glass over, splashing its contents all over the wooden bar top.

"Man down," I said. "Damn it, man."

A flush of embarrassment and self-consciousness joined the vodka blush I already had going.

I never felt as weak or pathetic as when I was drinking—and never practiced as much self-loathing—neither in volume nor vitriol.

"I'll get it," she said. "Just go sit down and I'll bring you and Frank a drink."

I turned toward Frank who was walking up.

"What're you drinkin', Frank?" I said. "Let me buy you a drink."

He held his hands up, palms out. "I'm good. Thanks though."

"Come on, man. Don't make me—don't be like that."

He nodded and gave a little frown of resignation. "A beer. I'll have a beer."

"Any particular kind?" I asked.

"Ah," he said, looking around, his eyes coming to rest on the Budweiser pendants hanging above the bar. "I'll have a Budweiser."

"The king of beers," I said. "Excellent choice. Draft or bottle? Margaret runs a full service drinkery here. She's no slouch."

Frank looked at Susan, who had drifted back over in our direction after passing out a few bottles and collecting the cash payments from guys who would become belligerent about their bills later.

There were no tabs at Scarlett's.

"Surprise me," he said. "No, you know what. I'll take a draft."

"You got it. How are you, Frank?"

"I've been better, but it's good to see y'all."

"You too," she said. "Always."

"Mind if I borrow your young man for a few minutes?" he asked.

"He's all yours. I'll be over in a minute with your drinks."

"Step into my office," I said, and stumbled back over toward what had come to be known as my table.

"How are you?" he asked as he sat down.

I nodded emphatically. "Really good. Things are great. You?"

I sounded like I was trying to convince myself as much or more than him, but neither of us was.

"Not so good."

"What's—"

"What're you—"

"You first," I said.

He looked down at my books. "What're you taking this semester?"

"Hebrew. Hebrew Prophets. And Biblical Interpretation. Have an exam on the prophets tomorrow."

He nodded. "That's good. Glad you got back in school and are doing so well. I'm proud of you."

"Why are things not so good for you?" I asked. "You working the three missing girls?"

He nodded again. "It's four now. Another went missing last night. But how'd you know they were connected? Nothing in the papers to suggest we think they're—"

"Just read the accounts and connected the dots," I said.

"What dots? There were no dots."

Susan arrived with our drinks. A Bud draft for Frank. A cup of coffee for me.

"Ah, Miss, this isn't what I ordered," I said.

"It's the only drink we have for underage drinkers," she said and moved away before I could argue with her about it. Glancing over her shoulder she added, "Especially when our favorite GBI agent is on the premises."

"Cheers," Frank said and held out his glass.

"Cheers," I said, white porcelain clinking shaker glass.

I took a sip of the strong, black, unsweetened liquid and had the urge to spit it back into the cup, but swallowed it instead. "That is truly horrific," I said and turned up the cup and quickly downed the rest of the tepid drink as if it were a shot, trying not to taste it as I did.

"How'd you know the three women were connected?" he asked.

"They were all runners or—"

He shook his head. "Reports didn't say that and they're—"

"Paper said the first one was a runner," I said. "The subtexts of the other stories along with the pictures included indicated the other two were athletic, in shape. I assume all three either ran or walked and were abducted while they were out doing it. All three are of similar age, body type, backgrounds. All have a similar look. Is the same true of the fourth?"

He nodded and sighed. "Yeah. And you're right. They're

runners. Went missing while out for a run. The doer's got to be in great shape. We're talkin' seriously athletic women."

"That's probably part of what does it for him," I said. "The challenge. The risk. Hunting what he considers a worthy prey. Plus he likes hard bodies. He has a type. Definitely got a serial on your hands."

"But a serial what?" he said. "What's he doing with them? Raping? Collecting? Killing? If he's killing 'em where're the bodies? If he's collecting them . . . where's he keepin' them?"

"He's got his own place," I said. "With plenty of room to work and or cage them. Or you just haven't found his dumping ground yet."

"How would you like to help us find them—and him?"

Frank had always been supportive of my interest in investigative technique. He had facilitated my work on the Atlanta Child Murders, even though to him and the other members of the task force the case was closed. He had helped me more than I could even calculate on the LaMarcus Williams and Cedric Porter cases. He had allowed me to work on a few of his cases with him and had even made it so I could take the training and get certified in law enforcement. Perhaps best of all, he had made it possible for me to attend some of the special FBI training at a few of their road school programs at various agencies in the area.

He was also the closest thing I had to a dad in Atlanta—maybe anywhere since my fractured relationship with my own father was still strained.

"How?" I asked, a jangle of electricity humming through me.

"Join the task force. You'd actually become an officer with one of the little towns around here—whoever has an opening. I'm still working out all the details. The job itself won't be anything special. You'll start out as a uniform, but you'd be on special assignment, working this case. You could stay in school, but you'd have to quit your job."

My jobs—janitorial work at the college and delivering Domino's pizza—were an embarrassment, and if he didn't know what they were I wasn't about to tell him.

"You've got a gift—think about how you connected the cases. We could really use it on this thing. Plus you're in shape. You still running?"

I nodded. Since I had stopped playing basketball because of what happened to Martin, I had started running.

"If this thing comes down to a footrace maybe you could actually catch the bastard. I'm not sure anyone else on the task force could."

"What happens when this thing ends?" I asked. "What if we catch him tomorrow?"

"You'd still be an officer with whichever PD we get you on with. Put in your time there and then you can transfer to Atlanta PD, one of the county sheriff's departments, or join me at GBI. It's all already arranged. All you have to say is yes."

"Yes."

"Yes?"

"Hell yes."

"You don't need to talk to Susan first?" he asked.

I shook my head.

"When can you start?"

"How about now?"

BLOOD STONE CHAPTER 2

I let myself into Cheryl Carver's apartment off of Wesley Chapel with the key Frank had given me, one of Frank's .45s in a holster on my hip, a penlight in one hand, the case file in the other.

What I didn't have was any kind of official ID, so I was hoping not to have any encounters with family, friends, nosy neighbors, or a zealous superintendent investigating suspicious activity in a missing woman's apartment.

The small, dark dwelling smelled stale, as if the still air trapped inside it hadn't been stirred in several days.

Beneath the staleness, the smells of everyone who had ever lived here lingered—layered, pungent, contradicting, steeped in the carpet, baked into the sheetrock, soaked into the linoleum.

Barely bigger than a studio, the tiny one-bedroom unit consisted of a small living room, a tiny kitchen and eating area, a prison-cell-sized bathroom, and a bedroom not large enough to accommodate even a queen-size bed.

And though there wasn't room for much furniture in the sad, desperate little quarters, there was room for far more than she had.

A single, old couch with a bunched and gathered slipcover on it was the only object in the living room. No TV. No coffee table. No chairs. No end tables.

A single framed photograph hung on the wall—a dime store or church directory family portrait portraying Cheryl and her younger brother with her folks, all of them dressed up, each coordinating with the other.

According to the file, Cheryl was from a small farming community in South Georgia and had moved to Atlanta for school, her track scholarship providing just enough to cover her classes, textbooks, and this minuscule off-campus apartment. A part-time job at Burger King provided both food and money for food.

A small folding card table with a single folding chair at it was in the dining area that fronted the one-cook kitchen.

The hallway leading to the bathroom and bedroom was lined with running ribbons and medals—marathons, half-marathons, track and field competitions, 5Ks, 10Ks, 20Ks, gold, silver, and bronze medals, blue, red, and green ribbons, but mostly blue ribbons and gold medals.

Cheryl had been raised in poverty, but was running away from it as fast as her long legs would carry her.

The small bedroom at the end of the short hall held a little girl's white pressboard twin bed with a juvenile pink bedspread, which I suspected had come from Cheryl's childhood bedroom, probably packed in the back of her dad's pickup truck and driven up from South Georgia with her mom's promise to replace it just as soon as she could save up enough to do so.

A small matching dresser close by held her bras and panties and socks and t-shirts and pajamas, its bottom drawer reserved for newspaper clippings of her races, random pictures of family and friends, and various cards and letters—mostly from her mom.

Unlike the rest of the apartment, Cheryl's bedroom still had the hint of fragrant flowers in it. Perhaps it was her perfume or body lotion lingering from where it wafted around her before she left, or the homemade lavender sachets in her closet and dresser drawers.

Very few clothes hung in the closet, mostly faded Sears and K-Mart shirts and well-worn off-brand blue jeans, jogging suits, and athletic attire, the floor beneath them littered with tennis shoes and track cleats that had traveled many, many miles.

I searched the room, looking beneath the bed, behind the dresser, under and around and in everything. There was nothing hidden. Cheryl Carver had nothing to hide.

From every indication she was living a Spartan existence, partly because she had no other choice, but partly because she was a disciplined dogged athlete, a dedicated and determined student.

Unbidden, thoughts of my own excesses floated to the surface of my still not completely sober mind.

Cheryl Carver had nearly all of her adult life ahead of her, and she was investing toward making it a good one.

And then she had encountered a madman.

A sadistic, heartless, heretic of humanity who derived pleasure from pain.

And for some reason she had not been able to outrun him. Was it because of the nature of his attack? Did he surprise her? Did he pounce before she even had the chance to run? Or, like her, did he too run like he was designed to?

I sat on the edge of Cheryl's small bed and took in more of her room.

The small boombox beside her bed, the many cassettes and few CDs surrounding it. The stacks of textbooks on the floor, the smattering of romance novels mixed in. The Chariots of Fire one-sheet thumbtacked to an otherwise empty wall.

The sadness pressing down on me was overwhelming.

Why did the world have to be this way?

Why couldn't a gifted student and athlete go for a run without running into brutality and depravity?

"Where are you?" I asked, my voice sounding small and out of place in the quiet, feminine apartment. "Are you still in the land of the living? Are you his prisoner? Or in what wound in the earth are you buried?"

No response.

"I will find you," I said. "Either way. I promise you that. I'm gonna find the madman who did this to you too. I wish I could undo what he's done . . . but . . . it won't go . . . unpunished. You have my word."

BLOOD STONE CHAPTER 3

Susan and I were living together in an old farmhouse off of Flakes Mill Road near Ellenwood.

Though most of the farm had been divided up and sold, the house still sat on ten acres and had a huge multi-car garage in the back, which the owner's son had built and filled with various sport cars in differing stages of restoration when he had lived here.

The house was small and drafty and had neither central air conditioning nor heat, but the rent was cheap, the rural feel refreshing, and it was less than five miles from the college I attended.

When I pulled into the small semicircle gravel drive, I could see that the lights were off in our bedroom, which meant Susan had already gone to bed.

I could feel the familiar agitation rising inside me, the tension gathering in my shoulders.

Most days this time of night when we both got home was our first and often only opportunity to spend time together and make love and she knew it. She not only knew that but knew how important it was to me. I was growing frustrated and more than a little angry at her take-it-or-leave-it, nonchalance approach to both our time alone together and lovemaking.

Instead of going to all four victim's homes, I had only gone to one—the one that was the closest to our home—so I could get here around the time she did. And she knew it. I had told her what I was going to do and why, and still she had gone to bed.

And once she had gone to bed, that was it. She wouldn't be getting up again. She wouldn't welcome a visit from me into our room. She was sending a message.

I wanted her every night, but tonight, after experiencing the overwhelming sadness and loss of Cheryl Carver, I needed her, needed the warmth, affection, and connection of human interaction and intimacy, needed to feel her live heart beating beneath her bare breasts.

Immediately I began to try and work out how much vodka I had hidden in the house.

I would read the case files and work my way toward oblivion.

A makeshift office in an alcove of the second bedroom created by placing bookshelves across the opening served as my small study and library, and tonight, investigative war room.

Case notes, photographs, and newspaper clippings spread out across my folding table desk, vodka in a coffee cup, orange juice in a glass for cover, and radio playing softly in the background—at the moment Whitney Houston's Where Do Broken Hearts Go.

The case file didn't yet contain any information on Kathy Dady, the fourth young woman to go missing, only Cheryl Carver, Paula Nichols, and Shelly Hepola.

The pictures I had of the three women showed just how alike they were. All tall, lean, athletic, attractive without being classically pretty. They wore little to no makeup and had a certain purity and plainness about them.

"You have a type, don't you?" I said aloud to the still faceless madman. "Why? Where does it come from? Do they all look like the same woman? Are you really doing this to her? Over and over again? Do you see her instead of them?"

As Whitney gave way to Richard Marx's Hold On to the Nights, the cold October wind found its way through the varnished boards of the old farm house, and I slid my chair a little closer to the space heater on the floor.

Wondering where the women were crossing paths with their abductor, I checked to see if they were all from the same area or had the same profession or frequented the same places.

Cheryl was a student in Decatur. Paula was a secretary in Marietta. Shelly worked retail in Duluth. They didn't go to the same gym or church or clubs. They didn't attend the same high school or college.

From what was in the file there was no obvious crossing, no intersection where the women would have encountered each other or the inexplicable madness that snatched them from their lives.

Two of the three women were single, and seemed not to have a lot of friends. They appeared to be introverts leading quiet lives.

Shelly had a boyfriend and he would have to be looked at closer, but if this was what it appeared to be, it was more likely a stranger than an acquaintance of any of the women. Of course, likely is not definitely.

When I became aware of the radio again, Phil Collins was singing Groovy Kind Of Love.

As I sipped my way toward stupor I wondered where the women were. Were we dealing with a collector or a killer? Either way, where were they?

Did he have a hidden dumping ground or a basement filled with cells or cages?

I still couldn't see his face, but if I knew which one he had, knew exactly what he was doing with his victims—rape? torture?

murder?—I'd have a better sense of him. At least that was what I told myself.

T he next morning I woke to the sound of a loud alarm blasting George Harrison's I Got My Mind Set on You.

Which wasn't a bad song to wake up to.

I was still sitting in the chair from the night before, my head lying on my arms on the folding table that served as my desk.

Susan, who had already left for her other job, had brought the alarm clock in and placed it on the tabletop beside my head, which meant she had to unplug it, move it, plug it back in, then reset both the time and the alarm—all early this morning while trying to get ready and leave for work on time.

As I sat up, I felt not only like I had had too much to drink the night before but that I had slept sitting up in an old desk chair, my head on my folded arms on a table. I was stiff and sore, my head ached, my arms asleep.

But George's catchy, repetitive, remake compelled me to get up and get going.

Glancing around my small office space, I saw that Susan had straightened up some, returning the papers and photos to the case file, removing the cups and mostly empty vodka bottle, and picking up the various articles of clothing and shoes I had left on the floor.

Next to the case file were my textbooks and notebooks for class and a note that said she had made my lunch and left it in the fridge.

She was always doing things like this—things that provoked in me both guilt and gratitude.

I was flooded with shame and, not for the first time, wished I could skip ahead to be an older, wiser, better version of myself. I wanted to do better, to be better, and I knew I could, but I wasn't yet and it frustrated and embarrassed me.

Reaching over and tapping the Snooze button on the clock and silencing the song that would echo in my head all day, I pushed myself up and stumbled out of my office and into my day.

After driving over and running at Panola Mountain State Park, I found myself as I had far too often lately, at Jordan Moore's grave in Fairview Memorial Gardens, which happened to be less than a mile from my house.

The early morning sun had yet to burn the dew off the ground and the sweat on my body was quickly turning cold.

"I know I've got to stop coming," I said. "And I will. I know I will. I just don't know when yet."

As I looked at her headstone while I talked to her, I realized what an odd thing it was to do. Perhaps something of her body still remained beneath the earth, but the headstone had nothing to do with her or her life. And I couldn't help but wonder if I'd be better off going to some place we actually spent time together.

"Damn you for what you did," I said. "Damn me for still being hung up on you."

Miss Ida, Jordan's stepmom, stepped out from behind the stone statue of Saint Mark and said, "Goddamn the whole mess. Every last bit of it."

Ida Williams, a largish black woman perpetually in a traditional African print dashiki and head wrap, had a son who was murdered during the Atlanta Child Murders, and I had investigated it when I had first arrived in Atlanta back in '86. I had actually solved the case and figured out exactly what happened to little LaMarcus, but at a price I was still paying.

"Didn't realize you still came here," she said.

I nodded. "Just live up the road."

"Is she why?"

"Huh?" I asked, not following.

"Did you move out here to be close to her grave?"

I opened my mouth quickly, but nothing came out. I was unable to respond because I couldn't admit the truth and I couldn't lie to her.

"It ain't my business," she said. "I just care about you, boy."

"I'm not doing too good right now," I said. "But . . . I'm doing the best I can."

She nodded. "Same here," she said and paused a moment before adding, "All we can do."

"I . . . feel . . . so weak . . . so . . . I'm pathetic."

"You're neither of those," she said. "You're just hurting, son. Grieving. Give it some time."

"It's been some time already."

"Then give it some more. What else you gonna do? What the hell else any of us gonna do?"

ALSO BY MICHAEL LISTER

Join Michael's Readers' Group and receive 4 FREE Books!

Books by Michael Lister

Blood Sacrifice

Rivers to Blood

Burnt Offerings

Innocent Blood

(Special Introduction by Michael Connelly)

Separation Anxiety

Blood Money Blood Moon

Thunder Beach

Blood Cries

A Certain Retribution

Blood Oath

Blood Work

Cold Blood

Blood Betrayal

Blood Shot

Blood Ties

Blood Stone

Blood Trail

(Jimmy "Soldier" Riley Novels)

The Big Goodbye

The Big Beyond

The Big Hello

The Big Bout

The Big Blast

In a Spider's Web (short story)

The Big Book of Noir

(Merrick McKnight / Reggie Summers Novels)

Thunder Beach

A Certain Retribution

Blood Oath

Blood Shot

(Remington James Novels)

Double Exposure

(includes intro by Michael Connelly)

Separation Anxiety

Blood Shot

(Sam Michaels / Daniel Davis Novels)

Burnt Offerings

Blood Oath

Cold Blood

Blood Shot

(Love Stories)

Carrie's Gift

(Short Story Collections)

North Florida Noir

Florida Heat Wave

Delta Blues

Another Quiet Night in Desperation

(The Meaning Series)

Meaning Every Moment

The Meaning of Life in Movies

Sign up for Michael's newsletter by clicking here or go to

www.MichaelLister.com and receive a free book.

www.ingramcontent.com/pod-product-compliance
Lightning Source LLC
Chambersburg PA
CBHW031341020726
47499CB00005B/1355